CAPTAIN MACKENZIE CALHOUN
SCRAMBLED FOR HIS SWORD . . .

. . . which lay just a few feet away. It skidded past where he lay and he thrust out a desperate hand and snagged it, just barely.

His enemy, Ryjaan, raised his dagger and leaped toward where Calhoun lay wounded, a shout of triumph already bursting from his lips. . . .

STAR TREK®
NEW FRONTIER

BOOK FOUR

END GAME

PETER DAVID

POCKET BOOKS
New York   London   Toronto   Sydney   Tokyo   Singapore

An *Original* Publication of POCKET BOOKS

POCKET BOOKS, a division of Simon & Schuster Inc.
1230 Avenue of the Americas, New York, NY 10020

STAR TREK is a Registered Trademark of Paramount Pictures.

A VIACOM COMPANY

This book is published by Pocket Books, a division of Simon & Schuster Inc., under exclusive license from Paramount Pictures.

ISBN: 0-671-01398-X

First Pocket Books printing August 1997

10 9 8 7 6 5 4 3 2 1

POCKET and colophon are registered trademarks of Simon & Schuster Inc.

Printed in the U.S.A.

Captain's Log, Stardate 50927.2: A slight wrinkle has presented itself in our dealings with the Nelkarites. I am attempting to deal with the situation in a Starfleet-prescribed manner of diligence and patience.

First Officer's Personal Log, Stardate 50927.2: We are faced with a somewhat disastrous situation. We have brought four dozen refugees to the planet Nelkar, at the invitation of the Nelkarites, who agreed to give them shelter. However, the Nelkarites are now using the innocent refugees in a bizarre power play. This is a classic section C-5 hostage scenario which calls for careful handling, but Captain Calhoun has displayed nothing but intransigence. If Mackenzie Calhoun thinks he can simply write off the lives of four dozen hostages . . . and follow it up by bombarding a planet . . . I am simply going to have to set him straight on that. And if I fail, then God help me, I may have to try and assume leadership of the Excalibur *on the basis that Mac is simply not fit for command.*

LAHEERA

1.

THE REFUGEES FROM THE *CAMBON* bleated in fear as they were herded into a large auditorium. Pacing the front of the room was the woman whom they knew to be Laheera . . . apparently a high muck-a-muck in the hierarchy of the world of Nelkar. She looked at them angrily, her fury seeming to radiate from her in such a manner that it was measurable by instrumentation. Standing next to her was Celter, the governor of the capital city of Selinium, which was their present location.

One of the group's leaders, an older, silver-haired man named Boretskee, took a step forward and said with slow uncertainty, "Is there . . . a problem? We were about to be moved into our new homes when—"

"Yes, you could say there's a problem," Laheera said, making no effort at all to contain her fury. It was rather an impressive combination: the golden, almost angelic hue of Laheera combined with unbridled fury. "We have asked that the *Excalibur* provide us with a simple form of 'payment,' as it were. Compensation for the trouble that we are going to to provide you with a new home."

The refugees looked at each other uncertainly. Cary, who was standing next to Boretskee, said, "'Payment'? We, uhm . . ." She shifted uncomfortably from one foot to the other. "We had not been under the impression that any sort of payment was going to be required. We would . . . I mean, obviously, we would like to cooperate. Anything that we can do . . ."

Celter now spoke up. "We do not desire payment from you. You are merely—to be blunt—a means to an end. We are not looking for monetary gain, but rather a simple barter situation. We have what you desire—a place for you to stay—and the *Excalibur* has advanced technology which we find desirable. We give you what you need, and we're given what we need. All benefit."

"The problem is that the *Excalibur* captain has refused to cooperate," Laheera cut in. "He has made it clear that he does not care what happens to any of you. He cares for his rules and regulations and for his own foolish pride. That is all."

"Happens . . . to us?" Boretskee was now profoundly confused, but he knew he didn't like the sound of that. "In what sense do you mean . . . 'happens' to us?"

But now Cary, Boretskee's slim, brunette wife, was looking around, and a terrible suspicion was beginning to dawn on her. "Where is Captain Hufmin?" she asked.

"Ah yes. The fearless leader of the good ship *Cambon,*" said Laheera, dripping disdain. "I'm afraid that we had to make an example of him. Best solution, really. His incessant pawing of me was beginning to get tiresome."

"An . . . example," Cary said slowly. "You . . . you don't mean . . . you can't mean he's . . ."

"If the word you're searching for is 'dead,' yes, that's correct," Laheera said flatly.

There were gasps from among the hostages. One young girl, named Meggan, began to cry. The others were too much in shock to do much more than reel at the news.

Drawing himself up, Boretskee said sharply, "And now we're next, is that it? Is that how this goes? Unless the starship does what you tell it to do?"

"That is correct, yes," replied Celter. Laheera nodded in silent agreement as Celter continued, "Now listen carefully to me. You have one chance, and one chance only, to survive. Captain Calhoun has made it clear that he is perfectly willing to let you die. It is up to you to change his mind. If you do not, we shall kill you all. Is that clear?"

Boretskee took a step forward, his body trembling with rage. He was something of a scrapper, and his dearest wish was to tell Laheera and Celter and every member of the Nelkarite race to simply drop dead and do their worst. But then he saw the frightened look on his wife's face, and saw likewise the fear in the expressions of the other refugees, reduced to nothing more than pieces in a sick power struggle between the

Nelkarites and the *Excalibur*. And he could not help but feel that his was the responsibility. Calhoun had voiced apprehension about the Nelkarites, but Boretskee and Cary had insisted that taking the Nelkarites up on their offer was the right way to go. And now look where everyone stood. No, if anyone was going to do something about this mess, by right it had to be Boretskee.

"All right," he said slowly. "Let me talk to him." And, noticing the sobbing young girl, he nodded his head in her direction and said, "And her, too. Calhoun would have to be one cold-hearted son of a bitch to ignore the pleadings of a child. Between the two of us we should be able to get him to do what you want," and silently he added, . . . *you bastards.*

You bastard, thought Commander Elizabeth Shelby, but she didn't say it.

In the captain's ready room, just off the bridge, it was entirely possible that she didn't have to say it. She stood there, facing Calhoun, who was looking thoughtfully out his observation window.

"You're not really going to do this thing," she said.

"Is that an order or a question?" he asked, his purple eyes flickering in—damn him—amusement.

"You cannot simply abandon the refugees to the mercies of the Nelkarites. Furthermore, you cannot then exact some sort of vengeance by firing upon Nelkar."

"Why?" He seemed genuinely puzzled. "Which part?"

"The whole thing!"

"Indeed." He frowned a moment, and then started

ticking off examples on his fingers. "If I had forced the refugees to remain on the ship against their will, that would have constituted kidnapping. Kidnapping is against regs. So, in accordance with regulation, I allowed them to settle on Nelkar. As such, they are now part of Nelkar society. If the Nelkarites decide that they want to obliterate the refugees, that falls under their prerogative, as per the Prime Directive. Correct?"

Her mouth opened for a moment, and then closed. Grimly, she nodded.

"That leaves the question of firing upon the Nelkarites. The Nelkarites are endeavoring to perform extortion. Attempting to perform extortion upon a Federation vessel is a violation of Federation law. As captain of the *Excalibur,* I am the authorized representative of Federation law for this sector. I consider the populace of Nelkar guilty of extortion. Would you argue that they're not?"

"No," she said quietly.

"No reasonable person would. So they're guilty as charged, tried and convicted in absentia. I also have broad latitude when it comes to deciding upon a sentence. So I sentence them to photon torpedo barrage."

"There is no such sentence in Federation law," Shelby informed him.

"True, but that's the 'broad latitude' part."

She slammed the table with her open palms, much as he had done the other day. It caused the objects on the surface to rattle. "There's got to be another way," she said tightly. "There's got to be. This isn't a word game. This isn't a puzzle. This isn't a joke—"

"I know it's not," replied Calhoun, and for just a

moment he let the frustration he was feeling show in his voice. He ran his fingers through his dark hair in frustration. "You don't understand, Elizabeth. I've faced this sort of situation before."

She tilted her head slightly and looked at him in puzzlement. "During your Starfleet career?"

He shook his head. "No. On Xenex, when I was a teenager." He leaned against his viewing port, and for the first time Shelby noticed that he looked extremely tired. "The Danteri captured the population of a small village, marched the people out, and announced that they were going to kill them all unless we, the leaders of the rebellion, surrendered ourselves."

"And did you?" she asked.

He grunted. "Of course not. We weren't stupid. They would have killed us immediately. I wish you could have seen those people, those captives. Down to the smallest child, every one of them was filled with Xenexian pride. Their heads held high, their faces unflinching."

"And you just . . . just stood by and let them all be slaughtered?"

"No," he said quietly. "We attacked. We attacked the Danteri while they were in the village. As we expected, they tried to use the citizens as shields. And there were the Xenexian hostages, shouting loudly, 'Shoot through us! Don't let them hide behind us! Don't inflict that shame on us!' "

"But you didn't really shoot through them . . ." But then she saw the look in his eyes, and her voice caught. "My God, you did. You killed them all."

"No, not all. Most of them survived, a happenstance attributable to good aim on our part and the

Danteri clearly being unprepared for their strategy not to work. To do otherwise would have been to bring dishonor among the Xenexians. They were willing to die for the cause."

"Well, that's really great, Mac," said Shelby, beginning to pace. "That's just swell. But here's the problem: The people stuck on Nelkar aren't out to be martyrs. They're victims who just happen to be in the wrong place at the wrong time."

"As were the villagers," replied Mackenzie Calhoun. "They didn't live their lives eagerly awaiting a violent death. But they were chosen by oppressors to be made pawns. If you let people with that mindset bend you to their will . . . if you give in, even once . . . it encourages further such actions."

"And it disempowers you, because you know you can be manipulated."

He nodded. "Yes. I'm pleased you understand."

Shelby stroked her chin for a moment, and then said, "If you don't mind my asking . . . who gave the order? To shoot through those hostages, I mean?"

She knew the answer even before he said it: "I did."

"And how did that make you feel? Knowing that they might be killed when you opened fire?"

"I had no feelings about it one way or the other," he said quietly. "I couldn't afford to."

"And you have no feeling about these hostages now? These people trapped below us on Nelkar?"

"None."

"I don't believe that," she said flatly. "The Mackenzie Calhoun I know wouldn't be uncaring. Wouldn't be writing them off."

He had looked away from her, but now he turned to

face her and said, in a very quiet voice, "Then I guess you didn't know me all too well."

"That may have been why we broke up," she mused. Then, after a moment's further thought, she said, "Captain, there has to be some other way. Some middle ground. Some way to proceed between the extremes of simply writing off the hostages as lost, and giving in to the Nelkarites completely. Perhaps if you study precedents . . ."

"Precedents?" He had a slight touch of amusement in his voice, which for some reason she found remarkably annoying. "Such as . . . ?"

"I don't know specifically. Actions taken by other captains, other commanders. Some way that will enable you to find guidance. You have to find a way to work with these people on some sort of equitable basis."

"I understand what you're saying, Elizabeth. And there may very well be merit to it. Still, I—"

At that moment, his comm badge beeped. He tapped it and said, "Calhoun here. Speak to me."

"Captain," came Robin Lefler's voice, "we are receiving an incoming hail from the Nelkarites."

Calhoun cast a quick glance at Shelby, but she was poker-faced. "On my way" was all he said, and he moved quickly past Shelby out onto the bridge. His crew, although maintaining their professional demeanor, nonetheless looked a bit apprehensive. He knew that they had considered his pronouncement a short while ago to be somewhat disconcerting. The concept of sacrificing the hostages in the face of a greater concern . . . it was difficult for them to grasp. They were good people, a good crew . . . but, in this instance, perhaps a bit overcompassionate. It was not something that he could afford to let influence his decisions, however. "Put them on visual," he said crisply.

A moment later, the image of Laheera appeared, and with her was Boretskee.

"There are some people here who wish to speak with you, Captain," Laheera informed him. She nodded to Boretskee.

Boretskee looked as uncomfortable as a person possibly could. He cleared his throat loudly and said, "Captain, I understand that we . . . that is to say, that you . . . have been placed in a rather difficult position. I . . . we regret this inconvenience and—"

Laheera made an impatient noise. He tossed a look at her that could have cracked castrodinium, and then resumed what he was saying. "There are innocent people down here, Captain. People whose lives are depending upon what you will do next."

Laheera now spoke up. "And do not get any charming ideas about using your transporters to solve the difficulties, Captain. We've scattered the hostages throughout the city. They're at no one location from which you can rescue them. For that matter, if you attempt to lock on to our transmission and, say, beam me out so that I can be used as a hostage . . . they will be killed. You've said that, as far as you are concerned, they are dead, and you will act accordingly. We both know it is easy to say such things. I invite you, however, to look upon the face of the 'dead.'"

She reached out of range of the viewer and dragged

someone else into the picture. It was Meggan, the little girl with her hair tied back in a large bun, her eyes as deep as the depths of space.

Calhoun looked neither right nor left, did not look at any of his people. Instead he kept his gaze leveled on the screen. When Laheera spoke it was with grim defiance—and yet that annoying voice of hers, with its musicality, made her life-and-death terms seem almost charming to hear. "Now then, Captain . . . your stubborn nature might be slightly more reasonable when the depths of your situation become apparent. You have said that you will open fire on us if we slay the hostages. My question to you is: Do you really have the nerve to stand there and let us kill them? You have said that the *Excalibur* is on a humanitarian mission. What sort of humanitarian would you be if you followed the course that you have set out for yourself, hmm? So, Captain . . . what will it be?"

Calhoun seemed to contemplate her with about as much passion as he would if he were peering through a microscope and watching an amoeba flutter around. And then, very quietly, he said, "Very well, Laheera. You are correct. This is a pointless exercise."

"I'm pleased you are listening to reason."

But Calhoun had now turned his back to Laheera. Instead he was facing Boyajian, who was standing at the tactical station, filling in for the absent Zak Kebron. "Mr. Boyajian," he said, and his tone was flat and unwavering. "Arm photon torpedoes one and two."

If Boyajian was surprised at the order, he was pro enough not to let it show. "Arming photon torpedoes, sir. Target?"

"Torpedo one should be locked on to the origin point of this transmission. Torpedo two . . ." He hesitated a moment, considering. "Run a quick sensor sweep on Selinium. Find a densely populated section of town."

"Populated?" Shelby spoke up, unable to keep the astonishment from her voice. "Sir, perhaps a technological target might be preferable? Some area of high energy discharge, indicating a power plant or—"

"Power plants can be rebuilt," Calhoun said reasonably. "People can't. Mr. Boyajian, have you got those targets locked in yet?"

"Yes, sir." Boyajian didn't sound happy about it.

"Projected casualty count from both torpedoes?"

Boyajian felt his mouth go very dry. He licked his lips, checked the estimates, and then said, "Ap . . ." His throat also felt like dust. "Approximately five . . . hundred thousand, sir."

All eyes were now on Calhoun. From her science station, Soleta's face was stoic and unreadable. At conn, Mark McHenry actually looked amused, as if he was certain that Calhoun would not do what he was preparing to do. Only Robin Lefler at ops was allowing her concern to show. She was biting her lower lip, a nervous habit that she'd been trying to break herself of for ten years. She wasn't having much success, and moments like this weren't making it easier on her.

And Shelby . . .

. . . Shelby was looking at him, not with anger, as he would have guessed, but with a vague sort of disappointment.

All of this, Calhoun took in in a second or two.

"Half a million. Impressive. Mr. McHenry, how long until we're in range?" he asked.

"At present orbital speed, one minute, three seconds," said McHenry, without, Calhoun noticed, checking his navigation board. Below them the blue/gray sphere that was Nelkar turned beneath them as they circled it.

"And once we've fired the torpedoes, how long until they reach primary targets?"

"Forty-seven seconds."

He nodded and then said to Boyajian, "Engage safety locks on the torpedoes, Mr. Boyajian. Forty-four-second cut-off."

"Engaging safety locks, aye, sir."

On the screen, Laheera watched the activity on the bridge without fully understanding what was going on. "Captain, what are you playing at? May I remind you we have the fate of the hostages to consider."

"There's no need. What you don't understand is that I am determining their fate. Not you. Me. And I'm determining your fate as well. Your earlier point is well taken. There's no need for me to stand around waiting for you to murder the hostages. For that matter, you've already killed one: Captain Hufmin. For that alone, you should consider this your punishment. A pity that others have to die with you, but those are the fortunes of war." And with what seemed virtually no hesitation on his part, he turned back to Boyajian and said crisply, "Fire photon torpedoes, and then give me a countdown."

For the briefest of moments, Boyajian paused, and then in a firm voice, he replied, "Aye, sir." He punched a control and two photon torpedoes leaped from the underbelly of the *Excalibur* and hurtled downward toward the unprotected city. "Torpedoes away," he said. "Forty-seven . . . forty-six . . . forty-five . . ."

It sounded as if Laheera's voice had just gone up an octave. Boretskee and the small girl were looking around in confusion, not entirely grasping what had just occurred. "What have you done?!" demanded Laheera.

"I have just fired two photon torpedoes. They'll be slowed down a bit as they pass through your atmosphere, but they'll still have sufficient firepower to level whatever they hit."

". . . thirty-seven . . . thirty-six . . ." Boyajian was intoning.

"You'll kill them! You'll kill her!" and Laheera shook the young girl, who let out a squeal of alarm. "You wouldn't!"

"Yes, I would."

"They're blanks! You're bluffing!"

". . . thirty . . . twenty-nine . . ." came the steady count from Boyajian.

"They're running hot, I assure you," he said with quiet conviction. "But they're armed with safety locks. I can abort them during the first forty seconds. In the last seven seconds, however, nothing can turn them back. Agree to release the hostages, or within the next . . ."

". . . twenty . . ." supplied Boyajian.

"Thank you, twenty seconds . . . you're dead. You, and about half a million Nelkarites. Gone, in one shot, because of the threats and strong-arming of you and Governor Celter for shortcuts. Decide now, Laheera."

For a moment she seemed to waver, and then she drew herself up and said firmly, "You are bluffing. I can smell it from here. Do your worst."

Calhoun's face was utterly inscrutable. "You're gambling half a million lives, including yours, on your sense of smell."

"Mine? No. No, I'm broadcasting from a deep enough shelter that I'll be safe. As for the rest, well . . . as I said, I'm positive you're bluffing. I'll stake their lives on my instincts any day."

"If you care about your people, reconsider."

"No."

There was dead silence on the bridge, and through it reverberated Boyajian's voice as he began the final countdown. "Ten . . . nine . . . eight . . ."

An infinity of thoughts tumbled through Shelby's mind. This was the time. This was the time to do it. For she knew now something that was previously unclear to her. Mackenzie Calhoun had spent his formative years as—simply put—a terrorist. It was easy to overlook that, because one tended to give him more flattering, even romantic labels such as "rebel leader" or "freedom fighter." But at core, he was indeed a terrorist, and he had fallen back on terrorist tactics. Proper procedures meant nothing to him. Life itself meant nothing to him. All that mattered was pounding his opponents until they could no longer resist.

". . . seven . . ."

Now, her mind screamed, *now! Take command, declare Calhoun unfit, and order Boyajian to abort! It's not mutiny! No one on this bridge wants to see this travesty happen! They're looking to me to take charge!*

". . . six . . ."

On the screen was Laheera, arms folded, smug, confident. The stunned, shocked faces of Boretskee and the young girl were evident.

". . . five . . ."

On the bridge was Calhoun, arms behind his back, staring levelly at the screen, and then, for no apparent reason, his gaze flickered to Shelby. Her eyes locked with Calhoun's, seemed to bore directly into the back of his brain.

Boyajian's lips began to form the letter "f" for four. . . .

"Abort," said Calhoun.

Boyajian's finger, which had been poised a microcentimeter above the control panel, stabbed down, the reflex so quick that he didn't even have time to register a sense of relief.

Several thousand feet above Selinium, two photon torpedoes—which normally would have exploded on impact—received a detonation command. They blew up prematurely, creating a spectacular flash of light and rolling of sound in the blue skies overhead. The people of Selinium—who had no idea that a pair of torpedoes had been winging their way—looked up in confusion and fear. No one had a ready explanation for what had just happened. A number of people had to be treated for flash-blindness, having had the misfortune to be looking directly into the explosion when it occurred. Many others had a ringing in the ears from the noise. Even as the echo of the detonation died away, Nelkarites turned to one another for answers and found none.

But an explanation was not long in coming. For Governor Celter immediately went on citywide comm channels and, with that famed, calming presence of his, seemed to be looking into the hearts of anyone who watched as he announced, "No doubt most, if not all, of you were witness to the explosion overhead. I am pleased to announce that we have been testing a new weapons system which will—I assure you—give us a new, more secure Nelkar than ever before. This was, however, a secret test, as such things often are, and we were not able to announce the test beforehand. On that basis, I hope you will forgive us any concern that might have been caused on your part. We are, after all, working for a common goal: the best, safest Nelkar possible. No need to concern yourselves, and you can all go on about your business. Thank you for your attention."

And he smiled in that way he had.

Once again there was silence on the bridge . . . except this time it was broken by low, contemptuous laughter.

The laughter was coming from Laheera. She could see the entire scene on the bridge of the *Excalibur*. It looked as if that Shelby woman was sorry that she couldn't simply reach through the viewscreen and strangle her. Still, Shelby's state of mind was hardly a major concern to Laheera.

Calhoun, for his part, stood straight and tall . . . and yet, somehow, he seemed . . . smaller.

"Now then, Captain," Laheera said, "since we know where each of us stands . . . let's get down to business, shall we? We can be flexible in our demands. Advance, in our weapons systems, in our warp drive propulsion . . . oh, and matter transportation, of course. We know that you've mastered it. Our experiments in that realm have been somewhat less than satisfying. Our test subjects have not come through the process in—shall we say—presentable condition. We trust that you will be able to aid us in these matters?"

"Yes," said Calhoun, in a voice so soft that it was barely above a whisper.

Indeed, Laheera made a show of cupping her ear and saying, "Excuse me? I didn't quite hear that."

"I said yes," Calhoun repeated, more loudly but with no intensity. It was as if there had been fire in him that had been doused.

"That's good to hear. Very good."

"We would like to . . . review the information that you need," Calhoun said. "Understand, this is not an . . . an easy thing we're doing. We still feel that giving you what you request is fundamentally wrong and potentially harmful. Obviously we have to cooperate with you, under the circumstances. But we want to try and minimize what we perceive as the damage we may do you."

"That's very considerate of you, Captain," said Laheera, making no effort to keep the irony from her voice. "After all, we know that at this moment, the Nelkarites are likely your very favorite race in the entire galaxy. Naturally you would be placing our welfare at the very top of your list of concerns."

Calhoun said nothing. There didn't seem to be any point to it.

"You have twenty-four hours, Captain. That should be more than enough, I would think. More than enough."

"Thank you," said Calhoun. "That's very generous of you."

She smiled thinly. "I can afford to be generous in victory . . . just as you appear to be gracious in defeat."

She snapped off the viewscreen and turned to face Boretskee and Meggan. "There," she said in that charmingly musical voice. "That wasn't so difficult now, was it?"

Boretskee's mouth drew back in a snarl. He was so filled with fury that he couldn't even form words.

"Now then . . . the guards will escort you to your quarters," she continued. "And there you will remain until we've gotten what we wanted. And if, for some reason, the *Excalibur* does not come through as promised . . . well then, we'll get together again," and she smiled mercilessly, "for one last time. Now . . . off you go. Oh, and have the guards be sure to take you past the Main Worship Tower. It's very scenic, and I wouldn't want you to miss it."

Shelby was prepared to console Calhoun in whatever way she could. To tell him that he had acted correctly. That in displaying mercy, he had shown strength, not weakness. That anyone else on the bridge would have done the exact same thing. That she was not ashamed of him, but proud of him.

She didn't have time to say any of it, because the moment that the screen blinked out, Calhoun turned to face his crew, wearing a look of grim amusement.

"'Gracious in defeat' my ass. I'm going to kick the crap out of them."

THALLON

II.

THALLON WAS A DYING WORLD . . . of this, the leader was certain.

The leader was in his study when the ground rocked beneath his feet. This time around, nothing was thrown from the shelves, no artwork hurled off the walls. It wasn't that the quake was any gentler than the previous ones; it was just that the leader, having learned his lessons from previous difficulties, had had everything bolted in place.

Still, that wasn't enough to prevent structural damage. The quake seemed to go for an eternity before finally subsiding, and while he was clutching the floor, the leader noticed a thin crack that started around the middle of the room and went all the way to one of the corners. His own, red-skinned reflection grimaced back at him from the highly polished surface.

He drew himself up to a sitting position, but remained on the floor long after the trembling had stopped. This place, this "palace" once belonging to the imperial family . . . it was his now. His and his allies'.

It was what he had wanted, what they had all wanted. What they had deserved. The royal family had ruled, had dictated, had hoarded, had been moved by self-interest for more generations than anyone could count. It was high time that the people took back that which was rightfully theirs. And if it benefited the leader, so much the better.

In a way, the royal family had led a collectively charmed life. Their ascension to power had its roots in the earliest parts of the planet's history, when they had been among the first to devise the Great Machines which had tapped into the energy-rich ground of Thallon. The machines' power had been theirs, and as the world had thrived . . . and later the empire had expanded . . . so had the influence and strength of the royal family spread as well. Indeed, the early stories of both Thallon's origins and the origins of the royal family were so steeped in legend and oral tradition that the world itself seemed to smack of mythology. It was as if there was something bigger-than-life about the homeworld of the Thallonian Empire.

But in recent years, as everyone on Thallon knew, the Great Machines were finding less and less energy to draw for the purpose of supplying Thallon's energy needs. Like an oil well drying out, Thallon was becoming an energy-depleted world. There had been cutbacks, blackouts, entire cities gone dark for days, weeks at a time. The legend had acquired a coat of tarnish, and that general feeling of dissatisfaction had grown and grown until it had spiraled completely out of control.

When wealth and power were plentiful, it seemed that there was enough for all. When such things were reduced to a premium, then did the remaining mongrels fight over the scraps. And the royal family had been torn asunder in the battle.

Many had already abandoned Thallon, the stars calling to them, offering them safer haven. There were, after all, other worlds within the once-empire that could sustain them. In addition there were places outside the empire to which they could go.

But there were others who refused to run. The symbol of their achievements was right here on Thallon. Indeed, many of them firmly clutched on to the idea that somehow, by dint of the royal family being dismantled, matters would turn around—that Thallon would be entering a new era thanks to the ejection of the royals—and there were many who did not want to take the chance of missing out.

And, unfortunately, there were a few—a precious few—who wanted the royal family back.

"You look preoccupied."

The leader glanced over and saw Zoran standing in the doorway. The tall, powerfully built Thallonian seemed to occupy the entire space as he stood there, staring in mild confusion and amusement. "Do you find it particularly comfortable on the floor?"

"In case you didn't notice, we just had another quake."

"Yes, I noticed. Nothing that any true Thallonian should be overly concerned about, though."

"You think not? Your confidence is most reassuring," muttered the leader, making no effort to hide his sarcasm. He rose to his feet and dusted himself off. "I am concerned that these quakes are going to continue to occur until . . ."

"Until what? The planet explodes?" Zoran made a dismissive noise. "Such things are the province of fantasy, not reality. This world is solid, and this world will thrive again. And you stand there and act as if it's going to crack open like a giant egg. You need to have a little more confidence."

"And you need to have a little less," said the leader. He began to pace, his hands draped behind his back. "I expected to hear from you via subspace radio. The lengthy silence was not anticipated."

"I felt it would be better to run silent," Zoran replied. "Transmissions can always be intercepted."

"Fine, fine," the leader said. "How did it go? Was the ambush successful? Was M'k'n'zy lured to the science station, as we anticipated?"

Zoran was mildly puzzled at the leader's attitude. He would have anticipated some degree of urgency in the questions, but instead the leader seemed barely interested. "No. The signal was sent out, as planned, and the *Excalibur* did receive it, but they did not show up."

The leader looked mildly surprised. "Odd. Ryjaan was positive that they would, as was D'ndai."

"Really." Zoran did not even try to suppress his smug grin. "And did either Ryjaan, the Danteri fool, or D'ndai, the idiot brother of M'k'n'zy Calhoun, tell you that Si Cwan was aboard the ship?"

The leader's face went a deeper shade of red as he stared in astonishment at Zoran. "Lord Si Cwan? He lives?" He seemed to gasp, his surprise apparently overwhelming.

"Not anymore. He and a Starfleet officer—a Brikar—flew out to the station on their own, in a runabout. Supposedly they were to provide temporary aid until the *Excalibur* could join them later, but what really caught Si Cwan's attention was that we listed his sister among the passengers."

"Why did you do that?"

"We thought that listing a member of the former royal family would be an additional lure and incentive for the *Excalibur*. We didn't want to take any chances of failing to catch their attention. Kalinda was the only one who is officially still listed as missing." He smirked. "One might consider it 'divine inspiration,' I suppose. I plucked her name out of the ether, and as a consequence, got the brother."

"You mean Lord Si Cwan is dead."

"That is correct."

"I see." He scratched his chin thoughtfully. "And it never occurred to you that if we disposed of him in a more public forum . . . say, here on Thallon . . . that it might better serve our interests."

"My interest was in seeing him dead. Period." Zoran was beginning to bristle a bit. "I would have expected a bit of gratitude from you. Some thanks. I tell you I wiped out Si Cwan, the man whom you hated more than any, and all you can do is stand there and make snide comments."

"No. That is not all I can do." And then, with a move so quick that Zoran didn't even see it coming, the leader's fist swept around and caught Zoran on the point of his chin. Zoran, caught off guard, went down. He sat there for a moment, stunned, the world whirling about him. From above him the leader said mockingly, "Do you find it particularly comfortable on the floor?"

Zoran's anger, barely controlled even at the best of times, began to boil up within him. "Why . . . why did you . . ."

"He's not dead."

"Yes, he is," Zoran said forcefully as he staggered to his feet. "I blew him up! Blew up the station! Ask Rojam if you don't believe me! Ask Juif! They were there!"

"Yes, I know they were. And so was D'ndai."

Zoran gaped. He could barely get any words out, and the one word he was able to manage was "What?"

"You heard me."

"He wasn't! He was nowhere around!"

"He showed up just as you departed. He wanted to check on your progress, to see if the *Excalibur* had fallen for the bait. He had intended to leave as quickly as he had arrived, but when he saw your hurried departure and no sign of the starship anywhere, he scanned the science station and discovered that there were two individuals aboard . . . and an energy build-up that indicated a bomb set for detonation. Since you had clearly deviated from the plan, he opted to take no chances and beamed them aboard his own vessel."

"They're safe?!" Zoran was trembling so violently one would have thought another quake had begun. "They're safe! I left them for dead, Si Cwan and the Brikar both! *They're safe?!*"

"No, they're merely alive. 'Safe' is a very subjective term. D'ndai has both of them in lockup on his vessel. He's bringing them here."

"Here! Why here?"

"Because," said the leader, and his voice became deep and harsh, "we're going to hold a proper execution. His will not be a fine and private death. All of Thallon will see the execution of Si Cwan. They will see him writhe, and cry out, and soil himself. There are some, you see, who still hold him in esteem. Still have an image of him as being a protector of the people, someone who cares about them. But I know him, you see, as do you. Know him to be as arrogant and insufferable as any of his brethren. And when the people see him wallowing in his own misery, then finally—once and for all—they will put aside all thoughts of their previous leadership." He clapped a hand on the shoulder of Zoran and smiled. "It will be glorious."

"Do you think that it will work out so easily?" asked Zoran. "Are people truly that easily manipulated?"

"The masses will believe what we want them to believe," replied the leader. "You would be amazed how easily people can be persuaded to accept whatever it is you want, particularly when you appeal to any of their four most basic motivations: Greed. Fear. A contempt for weakness. And self-preservation. When those are brought to the forefront of people's minds, governments topple, and the citizens congratulate each other and call themselves patriots."

LAHEERA

III.

THREE HOURS BEFORE she was confronted by a blood-thirsty mob, Laheera first learned that she had a serious problems on her hands.

She was in her office in the main government building. As military head and right arm to Governor Celter, she was naturally entitled to rather impressive quarters . . . not only in the main wing, but also in the subterranean shelter from which she was capable of conducting subspace negotiations with relative assurance of her own safety. It had been barely two hours since the communiqué with the *Excalibur* wherein she had signed off by congratulating Calhoun on being a gracious loser. She was busy trying to calculate how best to profit through acquiring the technology that would provide near-instantaneous matter transmission, when Celter had come running into her office. He slammed open the doors with his shoulder, barely slowing down, and his gold skin had gone completely ashen. "Have you heard what they're doing? What those bastards are doing? Have you seen? Have you heard?"

She looked up at him in confusion. "What are you talking about? What—"

"It's all over the comms! All over everything! Everywhere! Everyone's heard about it! You've killed us, Laheera! You've killed us all!"

He was becoming hysterical, words tumbling over each other, becoming impossible to understand. She rose from behind her desk angrily, crossed the room, and stood before him, arms folded impatiently. What she really wanted to do was slap him but, aside from slitting the occasional throat or blowing an opponent out of space, Laheera tried to avoid violence whenever possible. "Would you calm down and tell me what you're talking about?"

For answer, Celter pulled a remote off his belt, aimed it at her viewscreen, and thumbed it to life. The screen snapped on . . .

. . . and Laheera was seeing the bridge of the *Excalibur*. The angle was from over Calhoun's shoulder as he was facing the viewscreen . . .

. . . and she was on the screen. She was sitting there, conversing with Calhoun, and she was wearing an insufferably smug expression, and Calhoun was saying with a deadpan expression, "You're gambling half a million lives, including yours, on your sense of smell."

"Mine?" Laheera was smirking. "No. No, I'm broadcasting from a deep enough shelter that I'll be safe. As for the rest, well . . . as I said, I'm positive you're bluffing. I'll stake their lives on my instincts any day."

"If you care about your people, reconsider."

"No."

Laheera watched, feeling the blood drain from her face until her tint matched Celter's. Her mouth moved, but no words emerged, as the entire scene played itself out. Then the screen wavered slightly and the entire scene began again.

"Do you have any idea how this makes us look!" Celter was nearly shrieking. "There's the noble captain of the *Excalibur,* trying to save the hostages that we're holding . . . and yet valuing Nelkarite lives so highly that he preserves the lives of our citizens while we ourselves are willing to throw them away!"

"They were never in danger," Laheera tried to stammer out.

"Well, they don't see it that way!"

"Shut the picture off," she said, and when Celter didn't respond quickly enough, she grabbed the remote out of his hand and did it herself. She whirled to face him. "It's originating from the *Excalibur,* isn't it?"

"Of course it is! Where else?!"

"Jam it," she said tightly. "Jam the transmission!"

"We tried! They kept overriding it!"

"Shut it down, then! Shut down the entire comm system! Take it off the air!"

"We did that, too!" said Celter in exasperation. "We went dark over an hour ago! It took them no more than ten minutes to wire it back to life!"

"From *orbit?* What are they, magicians?!"

"They're devils! Devils incarnate!" Celter was wringing his hands. "There's uprising everywhere! The people are going berserk! They're furious! They say we don't care about them! That we used them, just as we're using the hostages!"

"We were trying to act in their best interests. . . ."

"I know that! You know that!" He pointed out in the general direction of the city. "But they don't know that! They don't care about it! They say we've betrayed them, and they're out for blood!"

"All right," said Laheera after a moment's thought. "Get to your personal broadcast studio. Get out onto the comm. Tell the people that this is all a trick. That the Federation is playing them for fools."

"They won't believe it," and he gripped her upper arm so hard that she felt as if he were going to dislocate it. "You haven't heard the things they've been saying. The rioting, the fury . . . I can't even get their attention. . . ."

"Yes, you can," she said confidently. Delicately she disengaged his grip on her. "That's always been your strength. Speak to them. Get out over the comm and tell them . . ."

"Tell them what?"

For a moment her patience wavered and she said, *"Something!"* Then she reined herself in and said more calmly, "Something. Anything. Just do it. And stop nodding like that!" Whenever Celter was particularly anxious, his head tended to bob in an accelerated manner. "You look like your head's about to fall off!" Celter grimaced and immediately gained control of himself.

Then he patted her on the shoulders, as if he were

drawing strength from her, and said, "Bless you, Laheera. I don't know what I'd do without you to help steady me." And then he hurried out of her office to prepare what he was determined would be the speech of his life. But he stopped just before he left and turned to Laheera, pointing a trembling finger. "And you . . . you get in touch with these *Excalibur* people. With this Captain Calhoun. We've tried to hail him; he ignores us. Perhaps he'll respond to you. You tell him we'll obliterate the hostages, every one of them, immediately!"

"I have that very thought in mind." She raised her voice slightly and said, "Okur!"

Okur was the name of one of the two guards who stood directly outside her office at all times. Okur was half again as tall as any Nelkarite that Laheera had ever met, and twice as wide. He was also her lover on the side; a nice way, she felt, of commanding loyalty. He took a step into the door, moving aside as Celter bustled out. He nodded slightly and said, "Yes?"

"Ready my safe room. And bring me Meggan. No others: just Meggan. I don't need any of the men attempting heroics. This time I'll cut her from sternum to crotch while Calhoun watches."

There had been no excess chatter on the bridge of the *Excalibur* for some time. Calhoun merely sat there in his command chair, fingers steepled, gazing intently at the planet below. "Lefler," he would say every so often, "how is it going?"

And she would say the same thing: "Broadcast continuing as ordered, sir."

He would nod, looking mildly distracted, and then go back to studying Nelkar, as if he were capable of actually seeing what was happening on the surface.

Speaking in a low voice so that only he could hear, Shelby leaned forward and said, "Mac . . . are you sure about this?"

He looked at her without answering, his purple eyes appearing distracted for a moment before focusing on her. Then he gave an ever so slight shake of his head before smiling widely. "I guess we'll find out together if this is a good idea."

Boyajian looked up and said, "Incoming hail, sir."

"Still from Celter?"

"No, sir. This is from Laheera."

"Ah." He rose from his chair, as if he felt some degree of comfort or even confidence by speaking to her on his feet. "Finally the power behind the power speaks to me again." He tapped his comm badge. "Burgoyne. Speak to me."

"Burgoyne here," came the voice of the Hermat chief engineer.

"As we discussed, Burgy. Are you at your designated post?"

"Ready and waiting for your order for emergency beam-out, sir."

"I'm keeping this channel open. Listen to everything that goes on and wait for my signal." He glanced at Shelby, who nodded back. "All right, Boyajian," he ordered. "Put her on visual."

The screen shimmered and Laheera appeared. With her, just as Calhoun suspected would be the case, was Meggan. Laheera cut straight to the point: "What did you think you were doing, Captain?"

He affected a blank look. "I have no idea what you're talking about, Laheera. Is there a problem?"

"Don't be disingenuous with me, Captain."

He turned to Shelby with what appeared to be a puzzled expression. "Polite word for lying," she explained.

"Lying? Me?" He turned back to the screen. "I am shocked and appalled that you would imply such a thing, Laheera. Here we are, working to give you the best possible opportunities as we submit to your demands. And your response is to insult me. You have no idea how hurt I am."

"This is a charming little dance you have, Captain," she snapped at him. "I know what this is about. You seek to even out the status quo. You feel I undercut your authority in front of your people. So you decided that it would only be fair if you returned the favor. I will not bother to offer any thoughts as to your actions, since I see no reason to give you even more fodder to confuse the good people of Nelkar. I want you to cease the broadcast immediately."

"Broadcast?"

She rubbed the bridge of her nose, her exasperation mounting. "Do I have to threaten you once more, Captain? Do I have to threaten her?" and she inclined her head toward Meggan. "Our instruments show the broadcast is coming from your ship."

"From *our* ship? An unauthorized broadcast? I am shocked and appalled. Lieutenant," Calhoun said stiffly, turning to face Lefler, "do you know anything about some sort of . . . 'broadcast'?"

Lefler made a great show of checking the ops board, and then she let out a gasp so loud that one would have thought she'd just been tossed into a vacuum and all the air in her body was being expelled. "Captain! We seem to have a problem with the BVL," and then, by way of explanation, she said to Laheera on the screen, "Bridge Visual Log," before continuing to Calhoun. "Apparently the Visual Log detailing your communication with Laheera has been set into some sort of automatic broadcast into the communications web of Nelkar."

"Good Lord!" declared Calhoun. "How could this have happened? This must be stopped immediately!"

"I'll get right on it, sir. I'll run a level-one diagnostic. I'll have this glitch tracked down in no time."

"Laheera," Calhoun said, turning back to the screen. "Please accept my most heartfelt apologies. This is a new vessel, and we're still working out many of the bugs. I must tell you that, having learned of this situation, I am, frankly, shocked."

"And appalled?" Laheera said dryly.

"Yes, absolutely, appalled. Far be it from me to risk stirring up the ire of your people."

"Captain, perhaps you think you are charming, or clever. But I am fully aware of your Prime Directive that states there must be no interference in planetary affairs. You are doing so now, and I insist that you cease all such interference. Or to put it in simpler, one-syllable words: Hands off."

"Interesting, Laheera," Calhoun said thoughtfully. "You want us to abide strictly by the Prime Directive when information being disseminated is not to your liking . . . but want us to violate it when it serves your convenience. You can't have it both ways, Laheera. And I wouldn't ask you to choose."

For a long moment the two of them simply stared at each other, challengingly, and then Laheera smiled. "Very charming, Captain. You seem to think you have proven a point. Perhaps I am now supposed to break down, admit the error of my ways, and remove the terms I have that govern the fate of these people," and she touched Meggan on the shoulder. Meggan shrank from her hand. "Captain, you are not in a position to try and enforce guilt on me, or make me bow to your desires." Something seemed to catch her attention, and then she said, "Governor Celter is about to address the people. I think it would interest you to see how a beloved leader can calm the concerns of even the most fearful of people."

She reached forward, apparently touching some sort of control, and then her image was replaced on the viewscreen by Celter. He was sitting in his office, looking quite relaxed in an overstuffed chair, his legs casually crossed. Calhoun could not help but be struck once more by the sheer golden beauty of these people. If only they weren't so contemptible and foul within.

"My good people of Nelkar," began Celter, spreading his hands wide.

That was as far as he got.

He jumped suddenly as the whine of a disruptor sounded outside the door of his office. He was on his feet, shouting out questions, demanding to know what was going on. It took absolutely no time for the answer to be supplied as the door was smashed open. Infuriated Nelkarites poured into the room, and if the faces of the Nelkarites looked nearly angelic when they were pleased, there was something incredibly

45

terrifying to see those cherubic visages twisted into pure fury. They looked for all the world like a heavenly host, come to wreak a terrible vengeance.

"No, wait!" he shouted. "We were never going to hurt you! It's not that we didn't care! We can work this out, yes, we can!" and his head was bobbing furiously in that manner which Laheera had found so annoying.

But they were not listening to him. They had already heard all they needed to hear. One of the mob was wielding a phaser-like weapon, and he fired. His aim was not particularly good, however, as his pencil-thin beam shot past Celter's head, missing him by a good few inches.

Celter, however, didn't see it, so distracted was he by the shouting and anger which filled the room. A Nelkarite wielding a club swung at Celter, and Celter adroitly dodged to his left. It was a quick move, and had the beam from the weapon not been there, he would have managed to avoid—at least for a few seconds more—serious injury.

But the beam was there, and since Celter didn't see it, the force and direction of his jump carried him straight through the beam, which sliced through his neck as efficiently as piano wire through cheese. Celter hadn't fully comprehended what was happening, and he was still nodding with desperate agreeability when his head slid off his shoulders and thudded to the floor.

There was a stunned silence on the bridge, and Shelby looked to Calhoun to see grim satisfaction in his eyes.

The screen switched back to reveal a shocked Laheera, who had clearly seen the entire thing. She was looking upward and to her left, apparently having witnessed the entire scene on another screen. Meggan had seen it as well, and she'd gone dead white, putting her hand to her mouth as if she was worried that she was going to vomit . . . which she very well might have.

Laheera looked straight at Calhoun, and then back at the unseen screen. And then it was as if she forgot that she was on a live transmission with the *Excalibur*. Instead she shouted, "Okur! Okur! Get in here!"

But there was no immediate response from the person she was trying to summon. Instead what she heard, as did the rest of the crew, was more sounds of shouting. Of running feet, and weapons being fired, and howls of pain and terror.

"People want to believe in their leaders, Laheera," Calhoun said quietly. "You betrayed them, put them at risk, were willing to write off half a million lives on a whim. People don't take kindly to such betrayals."

The door to her inner sanctum began to buckle inward, and Laheera let out a shriek. Meggan saw it as well, and she tried to bolt for a far part of the room, but Laheera snagged her by the wrist and whipped her around, holding her in front of her body as a shield. The child struggled as Laheera yanked out a knife—the same one that she had used to kill Hufmin—and put it to the child's throat. "Don't come in here!" she was shouting, although it was doubtful she could be heard over the torrent of abuse and anger that was pouring through the door.

"Captain . . ." Shelby said nervously.

Calhoun looked carved from marble. "You still on line, Burgoyne?"

"Still here, sir."

"Get ready."

On the screen, they saw the door bend still further, and then it burst inward. They saw a quick glimpse of Okur, and he was fighting with such fierceness that Calhoun had a moment of sympathy for him. Whoever this behemoth was, he was clearly not going down without a fight. There were cuts and bruises all over him, looking like obscenities against the pure gold of his skin. And then he did indeed go down, driven to the ground by the infuriated Nelkarites stampeding through the door.

"Don't move!" Laheera was shouting at the crowd. She pressed the knife up and against the child's throat. "Don't move or this one's death will be on your heads!"

And that was when Calhoun, calm as you please, said, "Burgoyne . . . energize."

And everyone watched as, on the screen, the familiar hum and scintillation of the transporter beams began to take effect. Laheera looked around in confusion as she heard the sound. Then she recognized it for what it was and for a moment—just for one moment—she thought she was about to elude her attackers.

She thought this for precisely as long as it took for Meggan's molecular structure to dissolve and be spirited away to the *Excalibur*. And then Laheera found herself holding her knife to thin air.

Laheera spun, faced the screen, looked straight

across the distance at Calhoun, and Laheera the blackmailer, the extorter, the murderer, screamed to Mackenzie Calhoun, *"Save me!"*

And it was M'k'n'zy of Calhoun, M'k'n'zy the savage, M'k'n'zy the warrior, who had crossed swords with an empire and lived to speak of it, who replied with icy calm, "You wanted hands off. You've got hands off."

The mob descended upon her, and just before she vanished beneath their number, she howled, *"You bastard!"*

He replied softly, as much to himself as to her, since she was otherwise distracted and unable to hear him. "You don't know the half of it. Good-bye, Laheera." He turned to Lefler and said, "Screen off."

Robin Lefler moved to switch off the transmission, but just before she could, she saw blood spatter on the picture. She jumped back slightly, as if concerned that it was going to spray on her. And then the potentially gory scene was replaced by their view of the planet below. It turned calmly, serenely, and from their godlike height it would have been impossible to tell that there was anything extraordinary going on.

"Commander," said Calhoun quietly, "give things an hour or so to calm down. Then contact the planet surface, find out who's in charge, and ascertain whether the safety of the refugees can be assured. Let's hope the new regime will be more reasonable. It's hard to believe they'd be less so." And he headed for the turbolift.

"If I may ask, sir, where are you going?" inquired Shelby.

He paused at the lift entrance and then said

thoughtfully, "To Hell, probably." And he walked out.

The bridge crew looked after him, and then Mark McHenry opined, "Give him six months, he'd be running the place."

No one disagreed.

Calhoun sat in the Team Room, staring intently at the drink in his hand. Crew members were glancing his way and talking softly among themselves. Word had spread throughout the ship of how Calhoun had handled the blackmail and threats of the Nelkarite government . . . correction, the former Nelkarite government. A general consensus had already formed among the crew: This was a man you definitely wanted on your side rather than against you.

"Captain . . ."

Calhoun looked up and saw Burgoyne 172 standing there. To Calhoun's mild surprise, Burgoyne stuck out hish hand. "If it's not too forward, sir . . . I'd like to shake your hand."

"Very well." Calhoun took the proffered hand and was astounded. Burgoyne's hand seemed to swallow his and, despite its apparent delicacy, the fact was that Burgoyne had one hell of a grip.

"I've served with a lot of Starfleet officers," said Burgoyne. "And many of them wouldn't have had the nerve to make the kind of calls you did. I have a knack for seeing things from both sides . . ."

"Yes, I just bet you do."

". . . and I just want to say that it's going to be an honor serving with you. An honor. May the Great Bird of the Galaxy roost on your planet."

Calhoun stared blankly at hir. "The *what?*"

"You've never heard of the Great Bird of the Galaxy!" said Burgoyne in surprise. "Giant mythic bird. Considered good luck, although," s/he added thoughtfully, "some races consider it a bad omen. But there are always malcontents, I suppose."

"Well . . . I'll take your 'blessing' in the spirit it's intended, then."

Burgoyne released hish hold on Calhoun and then strode out of the Team Room, leaving Calhoun trying to restore circulation to his fingers.

Shelby entered the Team Room and saw him seated off in a corner by himself. She walked slowly over to the table, nodding silent greetings to crew members as she passed them. Standing in front of him at the table, she couldn't even tell whether he was aware that she was there.

"Captain?" she said softly.

He glanced up. She remembered the first time she had looked into those eyes of his. One would not have been able to tell from her outer demeanor, for Shelby had already constructed the tough, no-nonsense, get-ahead attitude which she had considered necessary for advancement in Starfleet. But somehow those eyes had seemed to see right through it, as if no amount of artifice was sufficient to withstand his piercing gaze. Part of her was frightened. Another part was challenged. And a third adored him for it. And she was annoyed to discover now that her basic reactions had not changed, although she was doing everything she could to tone down the adoration part.

"You have a report, Commander?" he replied.

She nodded and sat down opposite him. "I've been

speaking to the new provisional governor. His name is Azizi. A little dour and downbeat, but basically a stand-up individual. He has given his personal assurance that the refugees are welcome to take up permanent residence on Nelkar. As a matter of fact, he's rather pleased with the notion. He considers them to be symbols of government folly. Of how people in charge can lose sight of truly important values."

"That's good to hear." He didn't sound particularly pleased. He didn't sound particularly anything, really. "And the refugees from the ship? From the *Cambon?* They're satisfied with this?

"They've already met with the new leaders. They're convinced that they're sincere. The fact that Azizi and his comrades have not asked us for anything certainly seems to reinforce their sincerity. As a matter of fact, Azizi has stated that Nelkar has a large area of unsettled land to the north. That if we wind up with more refugees in some future situation, we should feel free to bring them back to Nelkar and they will be accommodated. They're most anxious to make you happy, Captain. It, uhm," she cleared her throat in mild amusement, "it seems they consider you something of a hero."

"Fancy that. Very well then. Good job, Commander. I knew I could count on you to handle the situation."

"It's comforting to get the rare vote of confidence."

He looked at her with a slightly quizzical air, but she suspected the puzzlement was feigned. He likely knew exactly what she was going to say. "Anything else?"

"You did it again," she said. "Developed a plan and weren't honest with me about it. I didn't gainsay you when you decided to feed our record of the conversation to the Nelkarites. I rationalized that that was simply dissemination of information regarding already existing planetary situations. But you only said you hoped that the citizens would bring pressure to bear. You didn't say anything about a governmental overthrow."

"I didn't plan it."

"Oh, didn't you?"

"No," he said quietly. "I didn't."

"But you hoped for it."

"I hoped that the people would do what was right."

"What you felt was right, you mean?"

He smiled thinly. "That depends, I suppose, on whether you consider right and wrong to be universal absolutes, or hinging on one's perspective."

"You could have saved her. Saved Laheera."

"Yes, I could have."

"I thought that's what you had planned as a back-up, just in case matters did go over the top," said Shelby.

"Would you like a drink?"

"Don't change the subject, and yes."

He nodded, got up, and went over to the bar. He poured her a shot of synthehol and returned to the table, sliding it in front of her. She took it without comment and downed half the contents, then put the glass back on the table. "Well?"

"Well what?"

"Are you going to answer my question?"

"You didn't ask a question. You made a statement."

"I hate when you do this," she said, stabbing a finger at him. "I hate when you split hairs when you're in a discussion that makes you uncomfortable."

"You know me too well." He shifted in his chair, and then leaned forward. "I know you thought that was my backup plan. I let you think that. But I arranged with Burgoyne that, on my order, s/he would lock on to the origin point of the signal and beam up any non-Nelkarite life-forms."

"Leaving Laheera to face mob justice."

"At least it was some kind of justice," he shot back. "She committed crimes."

"We had no right to judge them."

"*We* didn't."

"Oh yes we did. Admit it, Mac. If we were in a similar situation, witnessing a violent governmental overthrow, and the person being overthrown was someone whose policies you agreed with, you wouldn't think twice about saving him or her. But with Laheera, you stood by and did nothing."

"Isn't that what the Prime Directive is all about?" he retorted. "Sitting around, doing nothing, tiptoeing around the galaxy and trying not to leave any footprints behind? I would have thought you'd be pleased with me, Elizabeth. I obeyed the Prime Directive."

"You obeyed the letter, but played fast and loose with the spirit. And dammit, you should have discussed it with me."

"I felt it would lead to an unnecessary argument."

"Maybe it would have led to a necessary argument." She leaned forward as well until they were almost nose to nose. "Level with me, Mac. Was her greatest crime that she murdered Hufmin and threatened the others? Or was it that she injured your pride? Called your bluff? Would you have let her live if you hadn't felt she made you look weak in front of the crew?"

He swirled the slight remains of his glass around in the bottom, and then said softly, "There has to be responsibility taken for actions. *That* is the galactic constant. There must be responsibility, and in this case, I forced it on Laheera."

"It wasn't your place to do so."

"Perhaps. Perhaps not. Sometimes you simply have to assess a situation and say, 'Dammit, it's me or no one.' And if you can't live with no one, then you have to take action."

"But . . ."

"Elizabeth . . . let me explain this with a visual aid."

She rolled her eyes. "Mac, don't patronize me."

"I'm not. I swear, I'm not. I just want to make a point." He picked up Shelby's glass and indicated the remaining contents. "Answer me: Half empty or half full?"

"Aw, Mac . . ."

"Half empty or half full?"

"All right," she sighed. "It's half—"

But before she could complete the sentence he tossed back the drink, then turned the empty glass over and put it on the table. And he said, "The correct answer is: It's gone. So why dwell on it?"

He handed her back the empty glass. She stared into it. "Thanks for the half a drink, Captain."

"My pleasure, Commander. We have to do this again sometime." He rose and said, "Have McHenry set course for the *Kayven Ryin* and take us there at warp four."

"Already done, sir. We're under way."

He blinked in surprise and glanced out the viewing port. Sure enough, the stars were hurtling past, space warping around them in a spiral of colors. "Ah. Nicely done."

"Clearly I'm going to have to read your mind, since you're being less than successful at communicating with me orally."

He nodded and started to walk past her, but she placed a hand on his chest, stopping him for a moment. "Mac," she said softly, "your self-reliance was always one of the things I lov—that I admired about you. It's probably your greatest strength. But you have to start trusting your officers. You have to start trusting me."

"I do trust you, Elizabeth."

"But you trust yourself more."

He shrugged. "What kind of captain would I be if I didn't?"

Shelby didn't hesitate. "The kind who would have saved Laheera."

For a long, long moment he was silent. Shelby was expecting some sort of smart-aleck reply, so she was surprised when he said, "Do you want to know what bothers me? Not this shadow dance or moralistic carping about justice versus compassion. Do you want to know what bothers me the most?"

"Sure."

He looked at her and there was something very terrible in those purple eyes. "I'm bothered that I turned off the screen. If I was going to refuse to save her, then I should have been strong enough to stand there and watch justice inflicted upon her. Instead I turned away. I let myself out. Oh, I tell myself that I was sparing my crew, but the truth is that I couldn't watch."

She wasn't entirely sure what to say. "Mac, I . . ."

"I used to be a strong man, Elizabeth. I keep this," and he traced the line of his scar, "to remind me of the man I was, because I was always concerned that life in Starfleet . . . life away from Xenex . . . would soften me. Would cause me to lose touch with my roots. And that's exactly what has happened. I made a threat, I was prepared to carry it out . . . and then I wavered. Then I carried out a plan that left a murdering bitch to her deserved reward . . . but could not watch. I've always told myself that I'm still M'k'n'zy of Calhoun, the barely contained savage wearing a cloak of civility. But what if, when you remove the cloak . . . there's nothing there?"

"Mac . . ." and she rested a hand on his shoulder. "You grew up at a time when compassion was a liability. A weakness. Now . . . now compassion can be your greatest strength. Don't be ashamed of it. Embrace it."

His reply was a grunt. "Let's agree to table this discussion, Commander."

"But—"

"No, Commander," he said in a tone that she had come to recognize. She knew there was no point in pursuing the matter as he continued, "Right now, my greater concern is Lieutenant Kebron and Ambassador Si Cwan. Let's hope their enforced time together at the *Kayven Ryin* was enough to make them think more highly of one another."

SI CWAN

IV.

"I hate you," said Si Cwan.

"Are you ever going to tire of saying that?" asked Kebron.

Deep in the bowels of the dungeons beneath the palace that was once Si Cwan's home, Cwan and Kebron were securely held. It had taken significantly more effort to keep Kebron in one place. While reinforced cable was enough to hold Si Cwan, Kebron was anchored with neural feedback inhibitors. The large electronic shackles amplified whatever energies he put into the cuffs that deadened all sensation in his arms and legs. Try as he might, he simply could not command his limbs to do what he wanted them to.

"I will tire of saying it when I tire of thinking it. First you fabricated that entire story about your parents in order to gain my sympathy. Then you were unable to help me overwhelm our captors . . ."

"We were outnumbered thirty to one," said Kebron. "There seemed little point to fighting them."

"Little point?" said Si Cwan incredulously. "Clearly they want to kill us!"

"If they want to kill us, why did they rescue us in the first place?" said the Brikar reasonably.

"Isn't it obvious? They want to make an example of me."

"Example?"

"They want to torture me and force me into making all sorts of confessions. They want to humiliate me, drag me down in front of the people of Thallon. To them I'm a symbol of everything wrong with this world."

"And aren't you? Tell me, Si Cwan . . . did you rule on your behalf, or on behalf of the people?"

"It's not that simple, Kebron."

"Perhaps," rumbled Kebron, "it should be."

Si Cwan sighed impatiently, clearly not interested in continuing the conversation. He looked around the cell and said, "You know . . . the irony of this is sickening."

"Really."

"Years ago, I allowed Soleta to escape from a dungeon cell . . . for all I know, this very one. So now I convince her to aid me in returning to my home . . . and I wind up in the dungeons. It goes full circle."

"Life often does," Kebron said.

Si Cwan tested the strength of his bonds. He pulled on them as hard as he could, but they seemed disinclined to give in the least. Kebron watched him impassively as, for long minutes, Si Cwan struggled, snarling and cursing louder and louder. Finally with an exasperated moan, Si Cwan sank to the floor.

"A very impressive display," Kebron said.

"Save the sarcasm, Kebron. It doesn't matter." And then, in a surprisingly soft voice, he said, "I guess none of it matters."

"Now *that* sounds somewhat defeatist."

Si Cwan seemed to have developed an interest in staring at his feet. "Kebron . . . what if I succeeded?"

"I'm not following."

"Let's say that I triumphed over my enemies. That the people rose up and supported me. That those who destroyed my life were, in turn, destroyed. Let's say that, once again, I was in power."

"I would assume that you would be pleased by that turn of events."

Cwan looked at him balefully. "It occurs to me that it would be as futile as pulling at these chains. Even if I wielded that power once more, I could not make my life the way it was. I could not bring my sister or any of the others back to life. I could do no more than create a shadow resemblance of my previous existence. I have my admirers, my supporters . . . but so what? For any rational, thinking person, there has to be more to life than that. There used to be, for me. But now there isn't."

"Si Cwan . . ."

"Besides, for every single supporter I may have, there are twenty who would just as soon see me torn to ribbons. People who, if handed a blaster, would aim it at me and pull the trigger themselves. I have spent my life trying to do my best, Kebron. And clearly it was not enough." He nodded slowly. "Let them torture me, I suppose. Let them do what they will. It doesn't matter anymore. None of it matters."

"And what of your enemies? You said that you didn't mind dying, but you were upset that Zoran would outlive you. Has that changed?"

"If I die before he does, or he before me, eventually we both end up in the same place. That's the odd thing about life. No one gets out alive."

Zak Kebron eyed him speculatively. "I must say, Cwan, I find this new attitude of yours rather annoying. You were more interesting when you were insufferable."

"I contemplate a life where I survive but know nothing but loneliness and memories of lost loved ones . . . or a life where I die after a battery of nauseating tortures. If those two possibilities render me 'annoying,' that's your problem, Kebron, not mine. You are merely a bystander in all this. If and when your vessel arrives on Thallon, they will likely release you to it with no difficulty. But I will be long de—"

The ground rumbled beneath their feet. Although Si Cwan was already seated on the floor, the force of the seismic shock sent him sprawling. Kebron, for his part, did not seem rattled at all. He merely sat there, looking—at worst—mildly vexed.

As the vibrations subsided, Si Cwan shook his head. "Now there's something to hope for: Perhaps the ground will simply swallow me up."

"Look, Cwan . . . you still grate on me," said Kebron. "Should we survive this, I doubt I will be any more inclined to feel friendship for you than I am now. Nonetheless, I dislike the notion of torture. So I promise you, you will not be tortured."

Si Cwan looked at him with a smirk that was, ever so slightly, condescending. "That's very kind of you to promise, Kebron, but I hardly think you're in a position to do anything about it."

At that moment they heard footsteps approach . . . a lot of them. The door to the cell hissed open and Si Cwan blinked against the sudden flood of light. There was a brace of guards there. The highest-ranking officer stepped forward, and he was smirking in a rather insufferable manner.

"Ah," Si Cwan said. "Hello, Herz."

"Hello, Si Cwan," replied the ranking officer. His speaking of Si Cwan's name was done in such a manner that it was clear he was enjoying the absence of any preceding title, such as "lord." "I'm flattered that you remember me."

"Herz was dismissed from our service," Cwan mentioned in an offhand manner to Kebron, "after two Vulcan prisoners escaped. Since the revolution, I see you are once again gainfully employed."

"Yes, no thanks to you. We have immediate plans for you, Si Cwan, and I assure you I have waited a long time for this."

"If what you intend is to take him to be physically abused . . . you shall have to wait a while longer," Kebron said. "You will not take him out of here."

There was something in his voice . . . something very certain, and very unpleasant. So unpleasant, in fact, that the guards seemed disinclined to get any nearer than they currently were. Impatiently, Herz said to them, "What are you standing there for? He can't break those neural inhibitors. Ignore him and take Si Cwan."

The guards started forward, and that was when Kebron began to focus his energy. With a grunt that reverberated throughout the room, he began to put pressure on the large cuffs. Immediately power started to ricochet back through his rock-like hide, but the Brikar either seemed to ignore it or, even more, to be spurred on by it.

"Stop it! You're not impressing anyone!" shouted Herz, trying to make himself heard over the accelerated howling of the cuffs. The fact was, he was lying. All of them were tremendously impressed. They were also having trouble hearing themselves think. The power surge was incredible, earsplitting; the Thallonians put their hands to the sides of their heads, assaulted by the intensity.

Si Cwan watched, wide-eyed, astonished, at the display of unrelenting strength. Kebron doubled, tripled his efforts. His muscles strained against his dusky skin, standing out in stark relief, and he was vibrating so violently that there might well have been another ground quake shaking the cell. Power coruscated around his body in an eye-searing display.

And then he broke the cuffs.

"Break" would actually be an inadequate description. With a roar that sounded more suited to a primordial beast, he shattered them, the bonds snapping under the strain, metal flying everywhere. One piece lodged in the thigh of an unlucky guard and he howled, going down. Another flew straight and true and thudded squarely into Herz's forehead. As it so happened, he was wearing a helmet. This was fortunate. Had he not been clad in that manner, the metal would likely have gone straight through his head without slowing. As it was, his skull was ringing, and it would only be upon removing the helmet later that he would discover the metal had stopped short of piercing his forehead by less than a centimeter.

"Fall back! Fall back!" he shouted, and the others did so, dragging the wounded guard with them. They stumbled back into the hallway and Herz punched a button on the wall that slid the door shut. It closed just barely in time as Zak Kebron slammed into it at full charge. The door, made of pure Staiteium, shuddered but held firm.

The guards' breathing came in ragged, disoriented gasps. Kebron, for his part, sounded utterly calm. "Listen carefully," he said. "Are you listening? I will only say this once."

"You're . . . you're not in a position to—" Herz tried to say, hoping to make up in bluster for his seriously crippled confidence.

"Be quiet," Kebron said impatiently. "I'm in exactly a position to do whatever I wish. If I put my mind to it, and pound on it long enough, I can get through this door. Or straight through the wall if I have to."

"You're . . . you're bluffing . . ." Herz declared.

"Apparently you have me confused with someone who cares what you think," Kebron informed him. "Now, then: There will be no torture of Si Cwan. He is not simply a former, fallen noble. He is a Federation ambassador. As such, he is entitled to certain courtesies under Federation law, including full access to the Federation embassy."

"What," and Herz looked at the others. "What 'Federation embassy'? There's no Federation embassy on Thallon."

"Yes, there is. This is it."

"That's not an embassy! It's a cell!"

"We intend to redecorate," Kebron informed them. "Now then . . . what with this cell being an embassy, you shall not be allowed to trespass here. This door does not keep me in. It keeps you out. If you attempt to violate this embassy, I shall take defensive action which will consist of ripping trespassers apart."

"We're in charge here!" said Herz unconvincingly.

"Out there, yes. In here, I am."

"You can't stay in there forever!"

"True. But we've no desire to. We shall stay until such time that the *Starship Excalibur* arrives."

"They don't know you're here!"

"I have every confidence in my associates that they will figure out where we are," replied Kebron, and indeed if there was any doubt within him, one could not have told it from his voice. "Once they have arrived, you will take us to them. And we will negotiate from that point. Now, kindly leave. The ambassador wishes to rest. It has been a trying time for him."

Realizing that control of the situation had completely spiraled away from him, Herz rallied himself and declared once more, *"That isn't an embassy!"* trying to make up in volume what he lacked in conviction.

Utterly composed, Kebron replied, "If you continue to maintain that attitude, we are not going to invite you to our first formal dance. And that, sir, will be your loss."

The wounded guard was still bleeding from where the metal had penetrated his leg, and the guards had decided by this point that further conversation was getting them nowhere. With a quick and angry glare over their shoulders, they hustled off down the hallway. Herz shouted defiantly over his shoulder, "This isn't over! We'll be back!"

"I await the challenge," Kebron called back. He peered after them through narrow slits in the door, watched them go, and then walked over to Si Cwan. With almost no effort at all, he snapped the bonds that had been holding Cwan. Cwan rubbed his wrists as Kebron stepped back and said, "So you fired that guard a few years back. I can believe that."

"How did you do it?" Si Cwan said, barely able to disguise his awe. "How did you break those bonds?"

"By refusing to fail."

Si Cwan shook his head. "I am impressed. I hate to admit it, but I am impressed. Now . . . let's get out of here."

"No."

Cwan was already halfway toward the door when he was brought up short by Kebron's curt answer. "What?"

"I said no."

"But we can break out!" Si Cwan said. "Unless you think you can't break down this door . . ."

"I probably can."

"Then we can escape from this cell!"

"And go where? You are the single most identifiable Thallonian on the planet, and I'll only blend in if there's an avalanche rolling down the main street."

He felt the old anger and impatience with the

Brikar welling up within him. "So you would give up."

"Not at all. We do exactly what I said we'd do. We stay here until the *Excalibur* shows up."

"This is the wrong way to go, Kebron. I'm telling you, we should leave! Now!"

"Very well," and Kebron gestured toward the door. "Go ahead and leave."

"But I can't get through the door!"

"That is not my problem."

With a roar of anger, Si Cwan waved his clenched fists in front of Kebron, until he realized the utter stupidity of such ire since Kebron was his only definite ally on the planet. And besides, hitting Zak Kebron was—at best—an exercise in futility. His fury spent, Si Cwan leaned against the door and murmured, "I hate you."

"Really. I saved you from being tortured."

"I know. That may be why I hate you most of all."

BURGOYNE

V.

BURGOYNE 172 WAS SCRUTINIZING the isolinear chip array, trying to determine possible methods of rearranging the chips to more effectively process sensor data, when s/he became aware of someone standing behind hir. S/he craned hish neck around and saw, to hish surprise, Dr. Selar. The doctor was maintaining her customary resolve, but it seemed to Burgoyne as if it was something of a strain for her.

"Do you have a moment?" she asked.

Burgoyne rose and brushed off hish hands . . . an old habit from the days when s/he would be up to hish elbows in various engine parts and have lubricant all over hish body. S/he missed those days more than s/he liked to think about. "For you, Doctor . . . two moments. Perhaps even three."

"I need to speak with you. Privately." She paused. "Woman to woman."

"You sure know how to hurt a guy," said Burgoyne. S/he gestured toward hish office. "After you."

Selar nodded and walked briskly to the office, Burgoyne following. The door hissed shut behind them and Selar turned to face Burgoyne. "I need to speak with you—"

"Woman to woman, I know. Doctor, you better than anyone should know I'm as much man as I am woman. . . ."

"Yes, and you've made your 'manly' interest in me quite evident. And Hermats are renowned for their rather cavalier approach to sexuality. . . ."

"I don't think I'd say 'cavalier,'" replied Burgoyne. "We simply see the opportunities inherent in—"

"Lieutenant Commander." Selar raised a hand, palm up. "I am really not interested in discussing Hermat philosophies right now, as endlessly interesting as I am sure they are. I desire you—"

Burgoyne sat up straight, a grin on hish face. "You desire me?"

"No," Selar said quickly, "what I am trying to say is that I desire *that* you . . . cease your efforts to pursue me on an amorous basis. I am aware of . . . indeed, impressed by . . . your remarkable affinity for pheromones. That you sense my . . . my interests. But I am asking you, as one officer to another, as . . ."

"One woman to another?" asked Burgoyne with just a touch of annoyance.

"Yes. I am asking you not to pursue me. There are . . ." Selar put a hand to her head to steady herself. "There are solid medical reasons why it would not be a wise idea."

"Even though I know we could be great together."

"Even though. I do not . . . desire a relationship. I have . . ." Selar cleared her throat, suddenly feeling as if she couldn't hear her own thoughts over the pounding of her pulse. "I have made a conscious decision to eliminate that part of my life. I am asking you to honor it."

"Eliminate it?" Burgoyne could hardly believe what s/he was hearing. S/he leaned forward and, to Selar's surprise, took the doctor's hand firmly between hirs. Burgoyne, for hish part, was surprised by the warmth. With the frosty, formal reserve of Vulcans, Burgoyne had somehow always just assumed that their skin would likewise be cold to the touch. Such was definitely not the case. "Selar . . ."

"Doctor Selar."

"Doctor Selar, putting my own considerations aside . . . that's no way to live. Even Vulcans have mates. Where else would little Vulcans come from? What happened to you? Something must have happened to make you like this. . . ."

Carefully Selar disengaged her hand from hish. "With all respect, Lieutenant Commander, it is none of your business. Nor is it any of your business why I am taking the time to ask you, specifically, to cease whatever amorous interests you may have in me."

Burgoyne took a deep, steady breath. And then, in an utterly formal tone, Burgoyne said, "Of course, Doctor. You merely had to ask. As a suitor, you need not worry that I will pursue you, amorously or otherwise." S/he paused, and then added, "As a friend, I'm going to make the observation that you seem a very sad and lost individual, and keeping the world at arm's length your entire life will just give you a long and lonely life, and tired arms."

"Thank you for your astute psychological analysis, Lieutenant Commander," she said. "Perhaps you missed your calling."

Ensign Ronni Beth knocked on the door to the office and Burgoyne gestured for her to come in. Beth entered and immediately said, "Sir, there's a problem with the ion flux. Also, Lieutenant McHenry is waiting outside. He says the ship is a little sluggish responding to the helm, and wanted to talk to you about it."

"I'm on it," Burgoyne said briskly, coming around hish desk. As s/he did so, s/he said gamely to Selar, "On the other hand, perhaps I didn't miss my calling at that." And, in a gesture that could only be considered friendly, s/he patted Selar on the shoulder.

The merest touch of Burgoyne's hand jolted Selar, filling her with a sense of electricity rampaging through her. It was all she could do to control herself. Burgoyne didn't notice Selar's fingers gripping the edge of the desk. "Perhaps not," Selar said, fighting to keep her voice even. It seemed to her as if she had barely managed to get the words out, and then Burgoyne walked out of the office and Selar sagged with relief.

She rose from the chair and walked toward the door with unsteady legs. As she crossed the engine room, she saw Burgoyne chatting with McHenry. No . . .

not just chatting. Laughing. Something had struck the two of them as amusing, and they were laughing over it.

And Selar felt jealous. She couldn't help it. She also couldn't believe it. Here she had come down to Engineering in order to put an end to Burgoyne's interest in her . . . and apparently she had succeeded, if one could take Burgoyne at hish word. Yet now, even seeing Burgoyne engaged in a casual conversation with someone else was enough to upset Selar.

"This is insane," she murmured, and she headed immediately to sickbay, hoping and praying that there would be someone sick up there to whom she could attend. When there wasn't, she felt like going out and breaking someone's leg so that she would have something to occupy her time and her mind.

Still, at least she was back in "her" place. Her home ground. Selar drew strength from sickbay. If she were prone to dwell on the irony of such things, she would have mused on the inappropriateness of garnering strength from a place of illness. But she wasn't feeling particularly philosophical at that moment.

What she was feeling was the drive of *Pon farr,* and it infuriated her that she could not get the image of Burgoyne out of her head.

At that moment her comm badge beeped. She tapped it and said, "Dr. Selar here."

"Doctor?" It was the captain, and he sounded momentarily puzzled. She couldn't blame him, really, because she realized that her own voice was deeper and throatier than usual, as if she had too much blood in her body.

"Yes, Captain," she said, reacquiring her customary tone of voice with effort.

"I just wanted to alert you to have sickbay ready. We'll be approaching the science ship *Kayven Ryin* shortly. Although at last report everyone there was fine, there may be some who need medical attention. At the very least, we'll want you to check them over and give them a clean bill of health."

"I shall be ready for them, sir."

"I expected no less. Calhoun out."

She leaned back and let out something that was very unusual for her: a sigh of relief. There would be something for her to do other than dwell on her own problems. Perhaps this would not be such a hideous day after all.

On the viewscreen before them, there was nothing but assorted scraps.

Calhoun rose from his chair, staring with sinking heart at the remains in front of them. "Are you quite sure we're in the right place, McHenry?"

McHenry nodded briskly. As was always the case with McHenry, while he seemed easily distracted or otherwise occupied mentally when matters were proceeding routinely, he was one hundred percent focused when there was any sort of problem. Indeed, one could almost take a cue as to the seriousness of a situation by how McHenry was reacting to it. Considering his no-nonsense demeanor at the moment, it was a serious situation indeed. "Yes, sir," he said. "Absolutely positive. This was the last point at which we heard from Kebron and Cwan."

"What the hell happened?" demanded Calhoun.

"Scanning remains," Soleta said from her science station.

"Remains. Remains of the *Kayven Ryin* . . . or of the *Marquand?*" asked Shelby.

It took Soleta a few moments, and then she said, "Both."

"Any signs of bodies?" Calhoun wanted to know.

"Yes. Mixed in with the wreckage, I am detecting two fingers . . . what appears to be a leg . . . a piece of bone . . . from the length, a thigh bone, I should th—"

"Soleta," Calhoun said sharply.

She looked up at him blandly. "I thought you'd want to know details."

"What I want to know is, is it our people?"

"Impossible to say at this time. I can have them brought aboard and analyzed . . ."

"Do it," Calhoun said briskly. "Lefler, oversee the operation. I want enough parts of the wreckage and the bodies brought aboard so that we know exactly what it is we're dealing with. Soleta, coordinate with Burgoyne. Go over the remains millimeter by millimeter if you have to, but I want to know what happened here. Bridge to sickbay."

"Sickbay, Dr. Selar here."

"Doctor, we're going to have need of your services."

"As per your request, Captain, I am prepared to handle whatever personnel are—"

"There's no personnel, Doctor," he said flatly. "I'm going to need you to perform autopsies. Actually, that might be too generous a word. I'm going to send you puzzle pieces and you're going to have to assemble them for me so I can get the entire picture."

Calhoun had a feeling that if he'd been face-to-face

with Selar, she would not have blinked an eye. He would have been correct. "Very well, sir. I will be ready."

"Captain," Lefler suddenly said. "There was another ship here. I'm detecting an ion trail."

He came over quickly to her, leaning over her station. "You think it's whoever destroyed the science station and the shuttle?"

"Possibly. By the same token, if we're going to be optimistic about it, they might have saved the lives of whoever was on the science station and the runabout."

"That is definitely optimistic, I'll grant you that. Can you determine the type?"

"Not at this time."

"Can you track it?"

She nodded briskly. "That I can do."

"Do it, then." He rose and turned to face his crew. "I want answers, people. I want to know what happened, so that when we catch up with whoever was the last person here, we know whether we're dealing with a potential ally . . . or avenging the death of two crewmen."

In the conference lounge, Calhoun sat at the head of the table. Grouped around him were Shelby, Soleta, Burgoyne, McHenry, and Selar. "So the ships were destroyed in two different manners?" he asked.

Soleta nodded, glancing at the computer upon which her analyses were appearing on the screen. "Yes, sir. The scorch marks on the remains of the *Marquand* indicate that they were destroyed by high-intensity firepower, although it is impossible to determine whether the science station itself was the origin of the attack. Now the *Kayven Ryin,* Chief Burgoyne believes—and I concur, with eighty-nine percent certainty—that the ship was destroyed by a bomb."

"A bomb?" Calhoun couldn't quite believe it.

"Yes, sir," Burgoyne spoke up. "A superheated thermite bomb, if I'm not mistaken, judging by the blast radius and chemical traces. I saw what one of those things did once to a surveying ship that wandered into Gorn territory."

"So somebody fired on the *Marquand* and then blew up the *Kayven Ryin.* Any guesses as to why or wherefores?"

"I dislike the notion of 'guesses,'" said Soleta. "If I had to reconstruct a scenario, I would say that the *Marquand* was ambushed within range of the science station . . . and then the station was subsequently destroyed, either to leave no clues as to what happened . . . or to kill whatever survivors there might have been aboard the station."

"Speaking of survivors," and Calhoun turned his attention to Selar, "what do the remains of the bodies tell us?"

"I have run DNA analysis. They are definitely Thallonian."

There was silence for a moment. "Si Cwan?" Shelby finally asked.

But Selar shook her head. "I do not believe so. Nor am I able to determine precisely what the cause of death was. Whether they were killed by the blast or before it is impossible to say."

"Any remains of a Brikar?"

"No, Captain. Not from what was presented to me."

Looks were exchanged around the room. Shelby asked, "Considering the density of Brikar hide . . . what are the odds that there would have been nothing detectable left of him?"

"If I had to estimate," and she considered it a moment, "seven thousand twenty-nine to one."

"That's impressive," Calhoun said slowly. "All right, McHenry," said Calhoun. "Have you got any bead on where we're heading? Where this 'mystery ship' has gone?"

"Well, obviously I don't know for sure where the trail ends until we get there," said McHenry. "But I tracked it ahead and, assuming that it didn't change course . . . we're heading straight toward Thallon."

"Thallon? Are you sure?"

McHenry nodded with conviction. "Yes, sir. I don't make mistakes."

"You don't?" Burgoyne said with amusement. "How very nice for you. I've never met anyone who doesn't make mistakes."

"I made a mistake once," McHenry said, but then he frowned and said, "No . . . wait. That time wasn't my fault. Sorry, my mistake. I was right the first time."

Wisely, no one commented.

"Well, we were supposed to go to Thallon," Shelby said after a moment. "Seems that we're getting there sooner rather than later."

"Indeed. Mr. Burgoyne, let's crank up the warp speed, shall we?"

"Ask and it's yours, sir."

"McHenry," said Calhoun, "best speed to Thal-lon."

"Yes, sir."

"And let's hope to Hell that Kebron and Cwan are there." He rose and clearly the meeting was over.

As they were heading out, Burgoyne said to Mc-Henry, "By the way, I think I've got that little problem taken care of. Let me know how she handles."

"Great. Thanks," said McHenry.

Selar looked at the two of them, realized that there were more unwelcome thoughts going through her head, and said in a low voice to Soleta, "I need to speak with you. Alone."

Soleta looked at her with mild surprise, but then nodded. "At my first opportunity," she said.

"Thank you." Selar looked around the now-empty conference lounge, and then said, "Soleta . . . I have never needed a friend before. But I need one now. I hope you will . . . indulge me." And she walked out quickly before Soleta could respond.

THALLON

VI.

IN THE MAIN COUNCIL CHAMBER of the Thallonian palace, the leader gaped at Herz. "An . . . embassy?"

"Yes, sir," Herz said, shifting uncomfortably.

Also in the room were: Zoran; D'ndai of Calhoun, the brother of M'k'n'zy of Calhoun . . . who, in turn, had not gone by that name in some time; and a new arrival . . . Ryjaan of the Danteri Empire. Ryjaan was squat and bulky, with bronze skin glistening with an even greater sheen than was typical for the Danteri. He had a ready smile, which had an additional tint of the sinister about it as his perfect teeth were slightly sharp.

Ryjaan had his hands draped behind his back and said, "Well, well . . . we've certainly got a muddle of this, haven't we? D'ndai, I ask you to take your brother out of action. But you . . . you don't have the nerve to handle it yourself. So you ally yourself with Zoran here, who sets up a trap for the purpose of doing what I asked you to do . . . except he doesn't wind up snaring your brother. Instead he snags a security officer and a fallen prince." He turned to the leader and said, "This is one charming alliance we've forged between ourselves, Yoz. The Danteri and the Thallonians, working hand in hand, creating a coalition that could eventually rival the Federation. And what have we got? A Federation starship commanded by an extremely dangerous individual . . . and a prisoner who has taken over his cell."

The leader, the one who had been addressed as Yoz, turned back to Herz and said angrily, "Drag him up here. Go in there with guns blasting and take him out."

"We, uhm . . . we tried that, sir."

"You did? And what happened?"

The door had flown open, packed with guards who were heavily armed, and they opened fire.

With a roar the Brikar had charged them. The blasts had slowed him, staggered him . . . but they had not stopped him. Si Cwan had remained safely behind the Brikar, and then Zak Kebron got his hands on the foremost of the assailants.

Soon the hallway was thick with blood, and it was all Thallonian. The guards had retreated, screaming, slipping and sliding on blood that was spilling everywhere, and Zak Kebron—as calm as anything—closed the door.

It wasn't the Thallonians' fault. They had not known that there were few things more dangerous than a

*wounded Brikar. Unfortunately, they had found out the
hard way.*

Yoz, Ryjaan, D'ndai, and Zoran listened in quiet
amazement. "Gods," whispered Yoz. Then he drew
himself up, his leadership qualities and conviction
coming to the fore. "All right. Gas them first. Don't
even enter. Just gas them from outside. Knock them
unconscious and haul Si Cwan out while the two of
them are downed."

"Uhm . . . we," and his voice sounded very faint.
"We tried that, too."

"And . . . ?" prompted Yoz.

*The door had flown open and the guards hesitated,
waiting for the thick clouds of gas to clear. They wore
masks so that they could breathe. Now they peered
carefully through the gas, trying to see where the
insensate bodies of Kebron and Si Cwan might be.*

*They were able to make out, over in the corner, a
fallen lump that seemed to have the general propor-
tions of Cwan. But at first they couldn't see Kebron at
all.*

Then they did.

*He had stepped forward from the mist, his mouth
shut tightly. They didn't see his fist, obscured as it was
by the mist.*

*Kebron's fist went straight into the lead guard,
striking a fatal blow. Then he raised the still-twitching
corpse over his head and hurled it into the crowd
of guards, knocking several of them back. He ripped
the masks off two of them, and then slammed the
door once again. The guards, Herz in the lead,*

*bolted down the corridor, not even waiting to hear the
clang of the door as it slammed closed once more.*

*It wasn't the Thallonians' fault. They had not known
that one of the only things more dangerous than a
wounded Brikar is a wounded Brikar whom one has
tried to gas into unconsciousness. Since Brikar can
hold their breath for twenty minutes at a stretch, that
was a useless maneuver. Unfortunately, they had found
out the hard way.*

Yoz turned to D'ndai and said, "I don't understand.
If Kebron was such a formidable fighting machine,
why didn't he do that on your ship? You said you had
weapons leveled at him, and he simply raised his
hands and didn't fight."

"It should be fairly obvious," said D'ndai. "He
wanted to find out who was behind all of this. He
wanted to get to the source of the situation. And now
that he's accomplished that, he's making his stand,
and waiting for my brother to come get him. And he
will, make no mistake. M'k'n'zy and his people will
show up. They won't believe that either Cwan or
Kebron is dead unless they have corpses to prove it.
And they will trace them here."

"Gentlemen," Yoz said slowly, "I am open to
suggestions here."

"Who gives a damn about the Brikar?" said Zoran
angrily. "Don't fiddle with gas to knock them out. Use
poison gas. Even if it doesn't affect Kebron, it will be
more than enough to obliterate Si Cwan. That's all
that matters! We have to kill him!"

"And is that your opinion, as well?" D'ndai asked
Yoz.

Yoz saw something in D'ndai's eyes. Something cool and calculating. "You feel that's not the case?"

D'ndai started to pace. "Yoz . . . my world fought a long war for freedom, against rather formidable odds. Every so often, the Danteri would foolishly . . . no offense," he interrupted himself as he addressed Ryjaan.

"None taken," said Ryjaan calmly.

"Every so often, the Danteri would capture a high-profile individual connected to our rebellion. They would make an example of him. They would execute him, usually in the most grisly fashion they could invent. Indeed, they'd try to outdo themselves every time. And all that happened was that they created martyr after martyr."

"What are you saying?"

"I'm saying, Yoz, that Si Cwan could be more dangerous to you dead than alive. You and your associates have thrown out the royal family, but you haven't consolidated your power. Chaos and rebellion are rife throughout what's left of the empire. Those who supported the rebellion may be starting to think that they were sold a dream, and the reality does not match the dream. If they see Si Cwan . . . if they see him die well, honorably, bravely . . . that could set forces into motion that you are not prepared for."

"So I was right," Zoran said sharply. "I should have killed him when he was out on the science station. For that matter, you should have killed him, D'ndai! You had the opportunity!"

"I'm not your hired assassin, Zoran. You were mine. If you bungle the job, it's not my responsibility to clean up after you."

"That's what you say," Zoran said in an accusatory tone. "Or perhaps you simply didn't have the stomach for it."

D'ndai smiled evenly. He bore a passing resemblance to his brother, even though the years had not worn well on him. "You are, of course, entitled to your opinion."

"What would you suggest, D'ndai?" said Yoz. "That we let him go?"

"No!" thundered Zoran, looking angry enough to leap across the room and rip out Yoz's throat with his teeth for even suggesting such a thing.

"No, I'm not suggesting that," said D'ndai. "I am suggesting he be tried, in an open court."

Yoz appeared to consider that, stroking his chin thoughtfully. "It has its advantages."

"Advantages!" Zoran clearly couldn't believe what he was hearing. "What advantages?"

"It puts us across as rational, compassionate beings," said Yoz. "If we beat him into submission and he agrees to whatever crimes we accuse him of, people are not stupid. It will reflect poorly on us. We do not want to appear simply as the greater bullies, the more merciless."

"But what crimes can we accuse him of?" asked Zoran. "There is no concrete proof of anything that he directly had his hand in."

"That much is true. But the activities of the others in his family, and in the generations preceding him, are public knowledge. Guilt by association."

"And there is . . . something else," D'ndai said slowly. "Something that I myself was witness to. I have been," and he looked around uncomfortably, "I have been reluctant to say anything until now, for I have no desire to disrupt the alliance between the Thallonians and the Danteri. Such a disruption could only cause difficulties for my people."

"Disruption?" Ryjaan seemed utterly confused. Nor did Yoz or Zoran comprehend either, as their blank looks indicated.

"There were," and D'ndai cleared his throat. "There were certain 'private' arrangements made. Certain allies that we Xenexians acquired when we were fighting for our freedom."

"What allies?" asked Ryjaan, and then slowly the significant look that D'ndai gave Yoz was enough to focus him on the Thallonian. "You?" he demanded. "The Thallonians allied with Xenex against us? *You!*"

Yoz threw up his hands defensively. "I knew nothing of it! You speak of matters twenty years ago! I was not even chancellor then!"

"Aye," agreed D'ndai. "Yoz speaks truly. He was not involved personally . . . not to my knowledge. But Si Cwan was."

"Si Cwan?" Ryjaan looked stunned. "But he was barely out of his teens at that time!"

"The same might be said of my brother," replied D'ndai. "And look at all that he accomplished."

"Zoran, did you know of this?" Ryjaan demanded.

Ryjaan looked to D'ndai, and for a long moment he was silent, wheels turning silently in his head.

"Well?" insisted Ryjaan. "At the time, you and Si Cwan were best friends. Did he mention anything of this to you?"

"No," said Zoran, sounding far more restrained than he usually did. "But there were any number of

times that he left Thallon for lengthy periods. When
he returned, he would never tell me where he'd been.
He was rather fond of his secrets, Si Cwan was."

"So it's possible."

"Oh, yes. Eminently possible."

"Very well," said Ryjaan, and he turned back to
D'ndai. "I appreciate your informing me of this
situation."

"It's more than just a situation that I'm informing
you of," replied D'ndai. "You see . . . I happen to
know that Si Cwan, in his endeavors to undercut the
authority of Danter, committed a variety of brutal
acts. One, in particular, will be of interest to you."

"And that one is . . . ?"

He folded his arms and said, "He killed your
father."

Ryjaan visibly staggered upon hearing this. "Wh—
what?" he managed to stammer out.

"You heard me," said D'ndai with supernatural
calm. "A high-ranking Danteri soldier named Falkar.
Your father, I believe."

Numbly, Ryjaan nodded.

"You understand, I did not make the association
immediately," D'ndai continued in that same, unper-
turbed voice. "But you and I have had continued
meetings, and since our alliance was becoming more
and more pronounced, I felt it helpful to—please
pardon my intrusiveness—explore your background.
I violated no secrets, I assure you. It was all information easily obtained through public records. But when
I learned that Falkar was your father, well . . . please
forgive me that it took me this long to tell you."

Slowly Ryjaan sank into a chair. "I was a child

when he left," he said calmly. "When he said that he was going to Xenex to quell a rebellion, he made it sound as if there was no question that he'd return. And he never did. His body was eventually recovered. He'd been run through, and his sword was never found. The sword of our family, gone. And all this time, I thought it was in the hands of some . . . some heathen . . . no offense," he said to D'ndai, with no trace of irony.

"None taken," he replied.

"You have no idea, D'ndai, how this unclosed chapter in my life has hampered my ability to deal with the Xenexians. I do so because it is what my government requires of me. But after all this time, to be able to resolve the hurt that I've always carried . . . the unanswered call for justice." He squeezed D'ndai's shoulder firmly. "Thank you . . . you, whom I, for the first time, truly call 'friend.' And when judgment is passed upon Si Cwan—when he is found guilty and is to be executed for his crimes—my hand will be the one that strikes him down."

And Yoz nodded approvingly. "We would have it no other way," he said. Then he considered a moment. "What of Kebron? The Brikar? He slaughtered a number of our guards. Are we to simply release him?"

"He killed fools," Zoran said with no sympathy. "Are we to publicly admit that a single, unarmed Federation representative obliterated squads of our armed guards? Rumors and legends of the might of the Federation are already rife throughout Thallon and the neighboring planets. Why provide them with even more fodder for discussion?"

"You're suggesting a cover-up then," said Yoz.

"I am suggesting mercy for the Brikar. After all, we have Si Cwan. We can afford to be . . ." and Zoran smiled, ". . . generous."

And as the others nodded around him, he exchanged looks with D'ndai. A look that spoke volumes. A look that said, *All right. I've covered for you. And you'd best not let me down . . . or there will be hell to pay.*

SELAR

VII.

SELAR STOOD ON THE CREST of Mount Tulleah, feeling
the hot air of Vulcan sweeping over her. It steadied
her, gave her a feeling of comfort. The sky was a deep
and dusky red, and the sands of the Gondi desert
stretched out into infinity. Selar had come to Mount
Tulleah any number of times in her youth, finding it a
source of peace and contemplation. Now, when her
world seem to be spiraling out of control, she was
pleased (inwardly, of course) to discover that Tulleah
still offered her that same, steadying feeling.

She heard feet trudging up behind her and she
turned to see the person she knew she would. "Thank
you for coming, Soleta."

Soleta grunted in response. "You couldn't have
been at the bottom of the hill?" she asked.

"One does not find spiritual comfort at the bottom of Mount Tulleah."

"No, but one does not run out of breath down there, either." She shook her head. "I have forgotten how arid the air is. I've rarely been to Vulcan."

"You do not know what you have missed."

"Actually," and she indicated the vista before them, "I suppose I do."

Selar shook her head. "This is an excellent reproduction, I don't dispute that. But in my heart, I know it is only that."

"In your heart. What an un-Vulcan-like way to put it."

"To court grammatical disaster . . . I have been feeling rather un-Vulcan-like lately."

"Selar," said Soleta, "you are in the early throes of *Pon farr*. If anything, you are a bit *too* Vulcan-like."

Selar stared out at the arid Vulcan plains for a time, and then she said, "I need to know what to do. I need to know what to do with these . . . these . . ."

"Feelings?"

"Yes, that is the word. Thank you. Feelings. I cannot," and she put her fingers to her temple, "I cannot get Burgoyne out of my mind. I do not know why. I do not know if the feelings are genuine or not, and it . . . it angers me. Angers me, and frightens me."

"Do you want to fight it, or do you want to give in to it?"

"Fight it," Selar said firmly. "I should be able to. I entered *Pon farr* two years ago. This is . . . this feeling I have now, I do not believe it to be genuine."

"Selar . . ."

"I know what you said to me. I know your assessment. But I do not think that what I am feeling is really *Pon farr*. Perhaps it is a . . . a delayed reaction to the death of Voltak. . . ."

"Delayed two years?" Soleta asked skeptically.

"Soleta . . . I profess to be an expert in many things. But emotions are not among them."

"Well," Soleta said thoughtfully. "I suppose it's possible. You were somewhat traumatized when you lost your husband. Perhaps, deep down, you desired to have that sort of connection once more."

"I resolved to divest myself of it," Selar said firmly.

"That may very well be the problem."

Selar stared out at the plains of Vulcan. "Burgoyne says s/he feels a connection between us. Says I am interested in hir. Perhaps s/he is right. Or perhaps my thoughts dwell on hir because s/he is the first individual who has ever shown that sort of interest in me. I do not know anymore. I do not know anything about anything."

"Admitting one's ignorance is the first step toward gaining knowledge."

"Thank you, Soleta. That still does not tell me what to do."

"I can't tell you that. No one can, except yourself."

Selar shook her head with as close an outward display of sadness as she ever came. "I have never felt any need to depend upon anyone except myself in my entire life. Perhaps . . . that has been part of the difficulty. I have been alone for much of my life . . . but until now, I have felt . . . lonely."

Far off in the distance, a flock of birds sailed through the sky on leathery wings. "I hope I have been of some help," said Soleta.

"Some. I still do not know precisely what action I will take. But at least I feel as if I am moving in some sort of a direction."

"That's all any of us can ask. I will be on the bridge if you need me."

Selar turned to her and said, "Thank you . . . my friend."

"You are most welcome."

Soleta turned and proceeded to climb down the mountain. Selar continued to look out over the Vulcan plains, but with half an ear she listened to Soleta's quiet litany of grunts, huffs, and muttered annoyance over the inconvenience of clambering up and down mountains. Within a few minutes, however, Soleta was gone, and Selar was struck by the fact that she missed her already.

She had so intensely desired to be alone, and yet she had to admit that she might have been craving a most unnatural state. Perhaps, even for Vulcans, loneliness was not a condition to which one should aspire. Perhaps there was more to life than isolating oneself, both intellectually and physically.

She found herself wishing that Vulcans truly were as many outsiders perceived them to be: emotionless. To have no emotions would be to simplify life tremendously. The problem was that Vulcans did indeed have emotions, but they had to be suppressed. Controlled. And perhaps she had gone too far in her effort to control all aspects of her life.

It was not surprising, she mused. After all, in addition to being a Vulcan, she had chosen medicine as her vocation. She was a doctor, and there was no breed who had to stay more in control, both of situations and themselves, than doctors. And so she never had any opportunity, nor any inclination, to relax and be herself with anyone. She always, first and foremost, had to be steering a situation. She could never give herself over to the natural movement of the event. In all likelihood, her aborted and awful experience with Voltak had soured her on that notion forever. After all, she had done that very thing, there in the joining place with Voltak. She had let herself be carried along by the currents of their emotionality, and the two of them had paid a terrible price for it.

And she had sworn that day never to let down her guard again, with anyone, for anything, under any circumstance.

But now it was finally beginning to dawn on Selar that there was a world of difference between being emotionally repressed and emotionally crippled.

Her natural inclination, as a healer, was to help those who were crippled, in any way she could. Now, looking to her own needs, she found herself reminded of an admonition from the Earth bible which one of the teachers had once mentioned to her. A saying that was particularly appropriate at this time:

Physician, heal thyself.

"Computer, end program."

The plains of Vulcan vanished, to be replaced by the glowing yellow grids of the holodeck wall.

"Physician, heal thyself," she said, and then left the

holodeck, although just for a moment she had the oddest feeling that she felt a faint wisp of a Vulcan wind on the back of her neck.

"Thallon, dead ahead, sir," announced McHenry. "Looks like they have some company."

That did indeed appear to be the case. There were several vessels already in orbit around Thallon. But only one of them immediately seized Calhoun's attention as he rose from his chair. "Son of a bitch," murmured Calhoun.

Shelby looked up in surprise. "Problem, Captain?"

"That ship there . . ." and he walked over to the screen and actually tapped on it. "Lefler, full magnification."

The ship promptly filled the entire screen. It was green and triangular in shape, with powerful warp engines mounted on the back.

Stepping away from her science station, Soleta observed, "That is a Xenexian ship, is it not, Captain?"

He nodded slowly. "It goes to show how quickly things change. When I lived there, we had no starbound ships. Our experiments with space travel were rudimentary at best. We weren't a starfaring race. Once we broke free from the Danteri, however, we began to take quantum leaps forward in our development. Sometimes I think it was the worst thing that ever happened to my people."

"The worst thing? Why?" asked Shelby.

He turned to face her. "Because I knew that we were getting help, and I never knew from where. It was a . . . rather sore point on the rare occasions when I came home. One of the main reasons I stopped coming home, as a matter of fact. But that's not just any Xenexian ship," and he turned back to the screen. "I recognize the markings on her. That's my brother's ship."

"Sir," Soleta spoke up. "The ion trail we were pursuing . . . it ends here. Not only that, but I believe that that vessel was the source of it."

"Hail her, Mr. Boyajian."

"Actually, Captain, they're hailing us."

"I suspected they would. Put them on screen."

A face appeared on the screen then, and Shelby was struck by the resemblance to Calhoun . . . and yet, by the differences as well. He looked like Mackenzie, but with a more self-satisfied, even smug manner about him. He inclined his head slightly and said, "Hello . . . Mackenzie." He overpronounced the name with tremendous exaggeration, as if it were unfamiliar to him. "That is how you wish to be called these days, is it not?"

"Where are my people, D'ndai?" Calhoun demanded without preamble.

D'ndai seemed amused by the lack of formality. " 'Your' people. I can see you making that reference to the rather large fellow in the Starfleet uniform . . . but am I to understand that Lord Si Cwan, former High Lord of the Thallonian Empire . . . is also to be grouped in among 'your' people?"

"I don't want to shadow-dance with you, D'ndai. Do you have them or don't you?"

"Have a care with your tone, little brother," D'ndai said sharply. "If it weren't for me, 'your' people would be nothing but scattered atoms right now.

Scraps for you to collect and keep in a jar. So I would have a bit more respect right now if I were you. Now," and he leaned back, looking utterly in control of the situation, "if you would like to come over here and discuss the matter of your missing crewmen . . . I would be more than happy to extend an invitation to you."

"Accepted," replied Calhoun without hesitation. "Calhoun to transporter room."

"Transporter room, Watson here."

"Watson, ready the transporter room. I'll be down in a moment and you'll be beaming me over to the vessel that we're currently in communication with."

"Aye, sir."

"Captain, I'd recommend a security escort," Shelby said immediately.

"Security?" Overhearing this on the screen, D'ndai actually seemed amused by it. "Are you overly concerned that I may harm you, Mackenzie? Has our relationship come to that?"

Calhoun was silent for a moment, and then he said to Shelby, "No security team will be necessary."

"But—" Then she saw his expression and simply said, "Aye, sir."

"I'll be there in a few minutes, D'ndai."

"We'll be certain to have out the good silver," replied D'ndai, and the screen faded out.

Before Shelby could say anything further, Calhoun turned quickly and said, "But before I'm going anywhere, we're going to find out what the hell is going on with our people. Soleta," and he turned to face her. "You said that the capital is called Thal?"

"Yes, sir. Last time I was there, in any event."

"Work with Boyajian and send out a message to them. I want to talk to whoever is in charge and find out if Kebron and Si Cwan are down there. If necessary, send an away team. I want to know what's going on with them, and I want to know now."

For the moment, matters were quiet at the Federation embassy, Thallon branch, Zak Kebron overseer and sergeant at arms.

The gas had cleared out and Kebron was sitting quietly, letting his body's impressive healing capabilities tend to the wounds that he had sustained. The fact was that Kebron was in more pain than he would have cared to admit, but the Brikar had a stoicism so renowned that they made Vulcans look like laughing hyenas in comparison.

It had been a while since Si Cwan had said anything as well. He sat on the far side of the cell from Kebron, his legs drawn up, his arms around his knees. Finally, he spoke up: "Kebron."

"What?" One could not have told from his reply that he was in any sort of physical discomfort.

"I . . ." He paused, and then continued, "I just . . . wished to say . . . thank you."

"You're welcome," replied Kebron.

After which point, nothing more was said. It didn't seem necessary.

Then they heard footsteps from the direction of the door of the cell. Slowly Kebron rose to his feet, a brief grunt being the only indication that he was starting to wear down. But from outside they heard a voice say, "Do not concern yourselves. There will be no battle. I am alone. No guards are with me."

Kebron noticed from the corner of his eye that something was wrong with Si Cwan. There was utter astonishment registering on his face. He looked at him questioningly, but it was as if Cwan had ceased noticing that there was anyone else in the "embassy."

"Do you recognize me, Si Cwan?" The voice came once again from outside the cell.

"You're dead," Si Cwan said, as if speaking from very far away.

"I was reported dead. One should never confuse reports with reality."

"Friend of yours?" Kebron asked.

Si Cwan looked at him with undisguised shock. "I had thought so, once upon a time." Then he called back, "Yoz? Chancellor Yoz?"

"Once Chancellor, yes. The tainted title given me by the oppressive royal family of Thallon, back before I saw the error of my ways and aided the people of the Thallonian Empire in throwing off the shackles of oppression."

"Save the rhetoric for the gullible," Si Cwan retorted. He was leaning against the wall, using it for support as he raised himself to standing. And as he spoke, his voice became increasingly louder and angrier. "Our trusted Chancellor Yoz. You helped organize the . . . the rebellion? You helped oversee the overthrow of the Thallonian Empire? You *helped destroy my family!? We trusted you!*"

"I was your flunky and you treated me with contempt. Don't endeavor to rewrite history now to suit your own purposes. I was always a second-class citizen to—"

And once more the ground beneath them shook.

This one was more violent than the previous occasions. Si Cwan stumbled back and fell onto Kebron, who managed to catch him at just the right angle so that he didn't injure himself against Kebron's rocky body. They could not see Yoz on the other side of the door, but Cwan took some bleak measure of satisfaction in the notion that Yoz was being flipped around helplessly. Kebron, unmovable, held on to Cwan and prevented him from rolling about more inside the cell.

And then something cracked.

They looked in astonishment as the cell floor shifted beneath them, and a large chunk of the ground actually cracked and thrust itself upward by about a foot. "I don't believe it," whispered Si Cwan. "What the devil is happening around here?"

Slowly the shuddering subsided. "Yoz," called Cwan. "Are you still with us?"

"Thank you for—" Yoz started to say, and then he coughed loudly. Dust was seeping in through the door; it was possible that new portion of the wall had crumbled outside, sending up waves of dust. "Thank you for your concern," he continued sarcastically. "I am here to inform you that your space vessel is here. An away team will be coming down to the People's Meeting Hall fairly shortly. You are invited to join us there. In order to do so, you will have to leave your 'embassy,' of course, but I guarantee you safe conduct."

"The 'People's Meeting Hall'?" inquired Si Cwan.

"What you used to call your throne room. All such artificial trappings are now in the possession of the good people of Thallon."

"It could easily be a trick," Kebron pointed out.

"Yes, your Commander Shelby said you might say that. She asked me to relay to you the following: Code Alpha Gamma Alpha. Does that have any significance to you?"

Kebron turned to Si Cwan and said, "It's no trick. We have regular security codes for identification purposes for just such situations."

"Situations such as this? That is impressively comprehensive planning."

"We are Starfleet. We endeavor to be prepared."

"So tell me, Yoz. Once I am brought to this People's Meeting place, what will happen to me there?"

"You will face your accusers," replied Yoz. "You will face the people of Thallon, and Thallonian justice."

"Very well. I accept your terms."

In a low voice, Kebron said, "I do not like this situation. You do not know what you are agreeing to. This could be some sort of setup."

"I agree," said Cwan. "But I do not see much choice in the matter, do you? I mean, as charming as these facilities are, and as pleasant as your company may be, I have no desire to spend the rest of my life in this 'embassy.' Do you?"

"I must admit that I had career and life plans which would be difficult to pursue from this location."

There seemed nothing more to say. Kebron walked slowly to the door and pulled on it slightly. It was not locked. He slid it open and, sure enough, there was only the Thallonian named Yoz standing there. Si Cwan came up behind Kebron and said slowly, "You know . . . I kept telling myself that if I encountered anyone from the happier days of my life, I would be overjoyed to see them. This simply goes to prove that nothing ever works out as one expected."

Rather than bothering to reply, Yoz instead made a sweeping gesture down the corridor. "It's this way," he said.

"I believe," Si Cwan replied icily, "that I know the way to the throne room . . . oh, I'm sorry. The People's Meeting Hall."

"How lovely that must be for you."

And as they started down the corridor, ex-Chancellor Yoz said, "Lieutenant Kebron . . . I apologize for your being dragged into all this. You are merely an innocent bystander in our planetary politics, and we do not hold you liable for any actions you may have taken as a result of our . . . disagreements. I trust we understand each other."

Kebron did not even look at him. He merely said, "Stay out of my way or I'll crush you like an egg."

Yoz stayed out of his way.

D'NDAI

VIII.

D'NDAI WAS WAITING for his brother in his quarters. The classic term for it was "home field advantage." But if Calhoun was at all discomforted by being on someone else's "home turf," he did not let on.

He looked around and nodded in what appeared to be approval. D'ndai's quarters were opulently decorated, with furniture that was both sturdy and also intricately carved. A large portrait of D'ndai hung on a wall, and Calhoun immediately recognized the style as one of Xenex's master portrait painters. "Well, well, D'ndai . . . you've certainly done well for yourself, haven't you?"

"That was always the problem between us, wasn't it, M'k'n'zy?" said D'ndai. "The fact that I have done so well for myself." He reached into a cabinet and withdrew a large bottle of liquor. "Drink?" he asked. "Far more potent and useful than that pale synthehol which I know is the beverage of choice on your starships."

"No, thank you."

"Why not, M'k'n'zy? Do you not trust my food or drink? What," and he laughed, "do you think I'm going to poison you or something?"

Calhoun smiled thinly and made no reply.

The silence itself was damning, and D'ndai made a great show of taking umbrage over it. "You cut me to the quick, brother. Such lack of trust! Such lack of faith!"

Ignoring his brother's posturing, Calhoun walked slowly around the quarters, surveying it. He rapped on the furniture, ran a finger along the edges of one as if he were checking for dust. "Where are they, D'ndai?" he asked, sounding remarkably casual.

"Are you going to thank me for saving them first?"

"Thank you for saving them. Now where are they?"

D'ndai took a sip of his drink and then said, "You know . . . in a way, I'm glad that you are back in uniform. It suits you well."

Each word from Calhoun was dripping with ice. "Where . . . are . . . they?"

"As it happens, they're on the planet's surface. I was going to be going down there myself within a few minutes. You are welcome to join me. We can see them together. They are healthy and unharmed . . . although not for lack of trying."

Calhoun cocked an eyebrow. "What do you mean by that?"

"I mean that, as much as I hate to admit it, the

Thallonians attempted some rather assaulting behavior on Messrs. Kebron and Cwan. These efforts were resisted, however. Your Mr. Kebron is a rather formidable individual."

"I will relay to him that you felt that way." He started to head for the door.

"M'k'n'zy! Don't leave so soon!" D'ndai called out. "There is much for us to discuss! Don't you think it about time that we did, in fact, discuss it?"

"And what would be the point?" demanded Calhoun angrily. Then he calmed himself and repeated, much more quietly, "What would be the point? You made your decisions. You know how I felt about them. What else is there to say?"

"I made decisions that benefited Xenex."

And this time Calhoun did not attempt to hold back his ire. Crossing the room quickly, his fists balled, he said tightly, "You made decisions that benefited you, D'ndai! *You!* You and the others!"

"Xenex has prospered under our guidance, M'k'n'zy. You know this. The people are happy."

"The people are miserable and simply don't know it!"

"And you do!" said D'ndai. He circled the room, speaking with his eyes thrown wide as if he were addressing the heavens. "You do! You know so much! You, M'k'n'zy, who went off to chart his own course and left us behind, know the state of Xenex's mind more than we do!"

"I left because I thought my job was done. Because I thought you could be trusted."

"And I could be."

"You sold out our people's spirit!" Calhoun said

angrily. "We won our independence from Danter, and then the first thing you do is arrange alliances and trade agreements with them!"

"We became partners with them. It's called advancement."

"We became slaves to them all over again! Oh, we were better kept, better pampered, but once again we were under the thumb of Danter! And this time we accepted it willingly! After twenty years we're right back where we started, and no one realizes that or understands it!"

"You keep saying 'we' as if you were a part of Xenex," D'ndai said quietly. "In case you've forgotten what uniform you wear, it seems to me that you, as an individual, have no say at all in the direction that our people have gone."

"Oh, I saw the direction it was going early on. I saw you in your meetings, your private sessions with the Danteri. I saw what you were up to, you and your cronies. I objected at the time."

"The war was over, M'k'n'zy. We won. Had we listened to you, we would have kept on fighting even when the other side was giving up. We would have become isolationist, cut ourselves off from opportunities." His presence seemed to fill up the room as D'ndai continued angrily, "When you were offered the opportunity to leave Xenex and gallivant around the stars, I didn't see you turning down that opportunity. But you would have had us turn away from a hand outstretched in peace that, once upon a time, would only attempt to swat us down."

"Don't you understand, D'ndai?" Calhoun said

urgently. "The triumph of Xenex was a triumph that came from within the souls of the Xenexians. We won our freedom without allies, depending only upon ourselves! Why was it then necessary to turn to our enemies for the purpose of maintaining that freedom . . . ?" But his voice trailed off as he saw something in D'ndai's expression. Partly it seemed like a self-satisfied smirk, as if D'ndai knew something that he wasn't telling. But there was also a hint of sadness in his expression. "D'ndai . . . ?"

"What makes you think we had no allies?" asked D'ndai.

"What?"

"M'k'n'zy, whether you're a Starfleet officer or not, you're still a fool. Of course we had allies."

"But . . ." Calhoun was confused, and for just a moment he felt as if he were no older than the nineteen summers he'd possessed when he'd first led his people to freedom. "I . . . I don't understand. What are you—?"

"Didn't you wonder where our supply of weapons came from? Our provisions when the Danteri cut off our supply lines? No . . . no, probably you didn't," said D'ndai contemptuously. "You were so busy planning strategies and anticipating the next move that the Danteri might make, you had no time to be concerned about any other matters. You were more than happy to leave them all to me. And I handled it."

"How?" And then, slowly, it dawned on him. "The Thallonians."

"That's right, M'k'n'zy. The Thallonians. There was no love lost between them and their neighbors, the Danteri. And when the Thallonians learned of our struggle against the Danteri, they were more than happy to supply us whatever we needed in order to keep that battle going. The matter was handled quietly; the Thallonians did not like to draw attention to themselves. But we had an alliance between us."

"And this happened without my knowing?" Calhoun couldn't believe it. "You should have discussed it with me! I had a right to know!"

"You were a teenager! An idealistic, battle-obsessed teenager, with more pride than the sky has stars. You would have fought to reject all offers of help. You would have disrupted everything, because you had a deep-seated need to handle everything yourself. I knew it would be the height of folly to tell you of our allies. I had no choice but to hide it from you. It would have led to unnecessary arguments."

"Or perhaps to necessary arguments!" shot back Calhoun. Then he paused a moment, wondering why those words sounded vaguely familiar to him.

Then he remembered. Remembered Elizabeth Shelby hurling practically the same sentiments at him. And he thought, *The irony of this is just sickening.* Rather than voice that sentiment, of course, he then asked, "But wait . . . how did we . . . you . . . become allies of the Danteri, then?"

"Because, with our being beholden to the Thallonians, we did not want to put ourselves into a position of weakness with them. By turning around and allying with the Danteri, it was a way of keeping the Thallonians in check. After all, we had no desire to have broken free of the Danteri Empire, only to find ourselves falling under the long arm of the Thallonian Empire. A sensible concern, wouldn't you say?"

"Very sensible. You always were the most sensible of men."

Calhoun stood there for a time after that, leaning against the ornate chest of drawers. D'ndai crossed the room, placing his drink down on the top of the chest, and he took Calhoun by the shoulders. "M'k'n'zy . . . come back to Xenex. You can do so much good there . . . more than you know. More than gallivanting around in a starship can accomplish. We of Xenex, we are your first, best destiny."

"Return for what purpose? So that I can fight you every step of the way? Or perhaps I'll simply get my throat cut one night in my sleep. That would not upset you too much, I'd wager."

"You wound me, brother."

"You'd do far worse to me and we both know it."

"I warn you . . ."

Calhoun stared at him, his eyes flat and deadly. "You're *warning* me? Warning me that my only chance is to become like you?"

Realizing that he was now treading on dangerous ground, D'ndai said quickly, "I know what you're thinking."

"No, you don't."

"Yes, I do. You're thinking that I've let down our people. That I, and the rest of the ruling council, sacrificed their interests for the various perks and privileges offered to me by the Danteri. That I am motivated by self-interest rather than general interest.

I can do nothing to change your perceptions except to say that, in my own way, I care about Xenex as much as you do."

"You see . . . I was right. You don't know what I'm thinking."

"Well, then . . . perhaps you'd care to enlighten me."

Calhoun's arm moved so quickly that D'ndai never even saw it coming. The uppercut caught him on the tip of the jaw and D'ndai went down to the floor. He lay there for a moment, stunned and confused.

"I was thinking about how much I would like to do that," said Calhoun.

"Did that . . ." D'ndai tried to straighten out his jaw while lying on the floor. "Did that make you feel better?"

"No," said Calhoun.

"So . . . you see . . . perhaps you have grown up after al—"

Calhoun kicked him in the stomach. D'ndai, still on the floor, doubled up, gasping.

"That made me feel better," Calhoun told him.

Soleta and Lefler stood on the flatlands outside Thal, Soleta with her hands on her hips surveying the area. Her tricorder hung off her shoulder, and there were a variety of instruments in the pack on her shoulders. She pointed to one area and said, "It was right there."

"The sinkhole?"

"Yes." She unshouldered the tricorder and approached the area which had, ten years earlier, swallowed her shuttlecraft. "This has been an annoyance to me for a decade. I landed my ship on an area that I thought was stable . . . and then it wasn't."

"Is that possible?"

"I would have thought not. But it would seem that on the surface of this world, virtually anything is possible." Lefler helped pull the backpack off her shoulders and then knelt down, beginning to remove instruments from the back.

Soleta walked forward slowly, the tricorder in front of her, taking surface readings. Behind her, Lefler was glancing over her shoulder at Thal, even as she set up a complex array of detection devices. The spires of the city were tall and glistening, framed against the purple skies of Thallon. But it was purely reflection of the fading sunlight. She remembered that, last time she had been there, the city was lit up. Not now, though. The lights were dark, to conserve energy. Energy that had always been in plentiful supply before the wellspring of Thallon had dwindled. "How do you think Commander Shelby and McHenry are doing over in Thal?"

"I am quite certain that they are handling the situation as well as, if not better than, can be expected. My concern is completing the job that I began ten years ago—namely determining the reasons for this planet's instability. An instability, I believe, which has only become more accentuated over the years. I also need to learn the origin of the energy that seemed to radiate from this planet's very core."

"My understanding is that they've been having a number of seismic disturbances as well," Lefler noted. She studied the sensor web array that she had assembled. "But what's odd is that initial sensor readings haven't detected any geological fault lines. So I'm not sure what could be causing them."

Soleta walked carefully, tentatively, around the area that had swallowed her shuttlecraft. Even though her tricorder told her that it was solid, she still found herself reluctant to take any chances. Although it was hardly more scientific than the tricorder, she reached out carefully and touched the area with her toe. It seemed substantial enough. She walked out onto it, like a would-be ice skater testing the strength of a frozen lake.

Meantime, the sensor web was anchored into the ground, sending readings deep into the surface of Thallon. They were the sort of detailed readings that simply were not possible from orbit. Lefler looked over the energy wave readings and shook her head in confusion. "I'm reading some sort of seismic . . . pulse," Lefler called. "That might be responsible for these shifts."

"A . . . 'pulse'? That's a rather vague term," Soleta informed her. "What's the cause of it?"

"Unknown. Don't worry, though. I'll get it figured out."

"I have every confidence that you will, Lefler. Just as I am confident that I shall figure out this curiosity with the fluctuation of the planet's surface."

"My my," said Lefler with amusement. "Nice to know you're so sure of yourself. It hasn't occurred to you, for instance, that maybe . . . just maybe . . . you accidentally parked your ship on a sinkhole and simply didn't realize it. And that the area you're looking over now is simply not the same place. You're asking me to believe that the ground out here is capable of turning from substantive to quicksand in no time at all."

"The alternative is that I am mistaken in this matter. That is highly improbable."

"Ahhh. Lefler's law number eighty-three: Whenever you've eliminated the impossible, whatever remains, however improbable, must be the truth."

"Lefler," said Soleta, her back still to her, "I'm certain that you consider this endless recitation of your 'laws' to be charming. Perhaps some people would share that opinion. To me, however, it comes across as a mere affectation, perhaps to cover up a basic insecurity. You feel that there are some areas in which you are not knowledgeable, and so you put forward authority in many areas. Even those about which you know little or nothing. Nor are these 'laws' necessarily of your own devising. That which you just quoted is, in fact, the noted 'great dictum' formulated by writer Arthur Conan Doyle in the guise of his literary creation, Sherlock Holmes. Understand, it is not my desire to upset you with these observations. Merely a concern that we are able to work together with a minimum of friction."

The only reply she received was silence. "Lefler?" She turned and looked in the direction she had last seen Lefler.

Lefler was gone. So was the sensor array.

"Lefler?" she called again. She took a step toward the area where Lefler had just been.

And Lefler's head suddenly broke ground.

The only thing visible was her face. Her mouth was open, her eyes frantic, and she barely had time to gasp out *"Soleta!"* before she vanished beneath the ground again.

Soleta charged forward while, at the same time, holding her tricorder in front of her. She scanned the surface and skidded to a half a foot away from the edge of the newly created sinkhole. She dropped to her belly and stretched her arm out as far as she could. She was two feet shy of where Lefler had vanished.

Moving as quickly as she could, Soleta stripped off her uniform, knotting the jacket and trousers together for additional length. For weight, she grabbed up a large boulder, tied the jacket around it, and then heaved the far end into the sinkhole while clutching the other end. Her major concern was hoping that she didn't accidentally knock Lefler cold with the boulder.

The lifeline, weighted down by the boulder, descended into the sinkhole. "Come on, Robin, find it," Soleta muttered. "Come on, come on . . ."

She knew that diving in after Lefler would, more than likely, be suicide. It was illogical for both of them to die. But it was what she was going to have to do. She steeled herself, reasonably saying a likely good-bye to life, and suddenly she felt a sharp tugging at the end of the lifeline.

Immediately Soleta backed up, pulling with all her not-inconsiderable strength. The line grew taut, and she prayed that the knots would hold. The last thing she needed was for the entire thing to come apart.

She backed up step by step, never letting up on the pressure, even though the sinkhole seemed to be fighting back. And just when she thought that Lefler couldn't possibly be holding her breath anymore,

Robin's head suddenly burst through the surface. She gasped, drawing in frantic lungfuls of air. Then, with herculean effort, she pulled one arm out of the mire and grabbed the lifeline. She pulled herself, hand over hand, until she was clear of the sinkhole, and then she flopped onto the ground next to Soleta, her chest heaving. It was a full minute before either of them was composed enough to say anything.

"I . . . think I found a sinkhole," Lefler finally managed to get out.

"So it would seem," replied Soleta.

"It appears the ground *is* that unstable. I'm sorry I doubted you."

"Well . . . do not do it again, and we should be fine. Fine, that is, as long as the ground doesn't dissolve under us again." She sat up, not having released her hold on the makeshift lifeline, and now she proceeded to pull it out so that she could unknot it and convert it back to its previous incarnation of her uniform. She examined her bare legs, badly scratched up by her lying flat on the surface, and then she glanced in the direction of the area where the equipment had been set up before being sucked under the surface of the planet. "So much for the sensor array."

"Actually . . ." Lefler said, and she held up the core data unit.

Soleta was surprised. "You managed to keep a grip on that even while you were sinking into the ground?" Lefler nodded, and Soleta said approvingly, "Very impressive."

"I'm nothing if not stubborn. We can get it back to the ship and analyze it there . . . right after we change into clean uniforms." As she looked over the data unit, she added, "By the way . . . I heard you starting to say something just before I sank. Something about my laws. What was it?"

Soleta hesitated a moment and then said, "Absolutely nothing of importance."

Commander Shelby looked around the crowded hall and couldn't help but feel how dangerously outnumbered she was.

She and McHenry had been seated in "places of honor" in the place called the People's Meeting Hall. Seated next to her was an individual who had identified himself as Yoz, and who appeared to be in some sort of leadership capacity. She could feel eyes upon her everywhere, as the Thallonians regarded McHenry and her with outright curiosity. A sea of red faces with nothing better to look at than two Starfleet officers. They chattered to each other in low tones while never once glancing away from Shelby and McHenry. Nearby her were two others who had been introduced to her as Zoran—who appeared to be some sort of aide-de-camp to Yoz—and Ryjaan, an ambassador from Danter. Ryjaan she had not met, but she knew of him; he had been present at the initial summit meetings which had resulted in the *Excalibur*'s assignment to this portion of space in the first place. Her eye caught a sword hanging from his belt, and he noticed that she was looking at it. "Purely ceremonial," Ryjaan said. "I'm expert in its use . . . but I've never wielded it in combat. With rare exception, we've evolved far beyond that."

"That's very comforting," said Shelby, not feeling

particularly comforted, particularly as the stares of the people of Thallon were getting on her nerves.

"I apologize for the curiosity of my people," Yoz said, leaning over to her and sounding genuinely contrite. He extended a bowl of what appeared to be finger foods.

"For a moment I thought it was just my imagination," she said. She took a sample from the bowl and ate it delicately.

"No, I am afraid not. We Thallonians are an interesting contradiction. We have an empire that spans many, many worlds. Technically a plethora of races constitutes the empire . . . or what remains of it, in any event. But Thallon itself has always remained somewhat . . . xenophobic. Visitors from other races, even those which are part of the empire, are something of a rarity on Thallon in general, and here in Thal in particular. And certainly for outsiders to be held in a place of honor . . . it is most unusual."

"I am most aware of that, Yoz. We've come quite a long way. Thallon has gone from being a world that shunned all contact, to a world that welcomes its first visitors from the Federation. And we appreciate it greatly."

"Do you?" Yoz was looking at McHenry with interest. "And does he?"

Shelby turned and saw that McHenry was staring off into space. She'd brought him along because he'd been working with Soleta on the history of the area. Now she prayed she hadn't made a mistake. McHenry may have seemed eccentric, but he always had a knack for rising above and beyond any occasion. She prayed he wasn't going to start backsliding now. "Lieutenant," she said sharply, and was relieved that McHenry immediately turned back to face her. "Lieutenant, I believe that Yoz was speaking to you."

"I was simply interested in your impressions of our fair city, Lieutenant McHenry," said Yoz pleasantly.

"Ah." McHenry, as he considered the question, bit into a greenish, curved, waferlike object from a bowl nearby. He smiled and looked questioningly at Yoz.

"Yukka chips. Thallonian delicacy. They're quite good."

"I'll say," agreed McHenry, crunching on several more as he thought a moment more. "Well . . . from my admittedly brief look around your city, and what I've seen so far . . . I'd say that you're all rearranging the deck chairs on the *Titanic.*"

"The . . . the what on the what?" He looked blankly at Shelby, who shrugged, and then back to McHenry. "I'm . . . afraid I don't understand . . ."

"Oh. Sorry." McHenry leaned forward, warming to the subject. "The *Titanic* was a huge Earth sailing vessel of several centuries back, considered unsinkable. It hit an iceberg and sank."

"I see," Yoz said slowly. "And to move furniture around on a vessel that is sinking would be an exercise in futility. An indication that one is in denial that the ship is going down."

"Exactly." McHenry nodded amiably. "I mean, we're here because the Thallonian Empire has collapsed, and you guys are sitting around here like you're about to rebuild something. Like, if you can keep everything together here on Thallon, you might somehow be able to keep going with the only change in status being that you guys are in charge instead of the other guys. It's not going to happen that way."

"And do you share the lieutenant's view, Commander?"

Shelby looked Yoz straight in the eye and said, "I might not have been quite as blunt . . . but I would say that his assessment is accurate enough. You have serious problems here, Yoz, and it seems to me that you're more concerned with putting on a show for the spectators than actually trying to address them."

"This 'show' that we are putting on *is* how we are trying to address them," replied Yoz. "We are endeavoring to show the people that the Thallonian Empire—which, by the way, we will be formally renaming the Thallonian Alliance—cannot, must not, descend into chaos."

"It already has, sir," said Shelby. "The trick is to extricate it."

"Very well, then. And the way that we will extricate it is to show that there is order to be offered. And one of the fundamental means of putting forward order is through justice. Would you agree to that, Commander?"

She was about to answer when she heard the familiar whine of transporter beams. There were surprised gasps from the people watching the proceedings. They had seen matter transportation before, but most transmat on Thallon was done with sending and receiving platforms. People materializing out of thin air was not a common sight.

The beams coalesced into two forms: Captain Calhoun and D'ndai, with the transporter beams having originated from the *Excalibur*. Both of them were staring fixedly straight ahead, as if they were determined to look anywhere but at each other. Calhoun saw his second-in-command and helmsman, and nodded slightly in acknowledgment of their presence. Then he walked over to Yoz and introductions were quickly made. More chairs were immediately brought over and Calhoun sat down nearby Shelby. He was surprised to find that he was practically sinking into the cushions, and had to readjust himself so that he would not disappear entirely.

"It is good of you to be able to join us, Captain," said Yoz amiably. "I was just having an interesting discussion with your first officer. A discussion about justice."

"Really?" Calhoun looked at Shelby with raised eyebrow. "I'd be interested to hear the outcome of that discussion myself."

"I was simply saying that justice, and the means by which justice is applied, is one of the cornerstones of a civilized society. And that is what we are trying to institute here. Would you agree with that, Commander?"

"I would," said Shelby reasonably.

"And that interference with that justice would be tantamount to endorsing chaos. Isn't that right as well?"

But by this point Shelby's "antennae" were up, and she saw by Calhoun's expression that his were as well. "I would be most interested to know where this is leading, Yoz," Shelby said.

"Very well. I will be forthcoming." He leaned forward and said, "We are about to bring out Si Cwan. As far as the current government of Thallon is concerned, he is an outlaw. He has had the temerity to reenter our space. We desire to try him accordingly. Will you interfere?"

Shelby wanted to respond, but instead she waited for Calhoun to say something. But instead he simply watched her, inclining his head slightly to indicate that she should go ahead and speak. "We have a law, called the Prime Directive. It pledges noninterference. If Si Cwan is in the hands of local authorities . . . there is little we can do."

"You would not simply transport him away if the decisions being made went against him."

"That . . . would not be permissible, no," she said slowly. She looked back to Calhoun, but his expression was stony and silent. "But may I ask what crimes he has supposedly committed against you?"

"Not just against his fellow Thallonians," Ryjaan spoke up. He seemed in an extraordinarily good mood. "Against the Danteri as well. He killed a high-ranking Danteri officer. For that alone, he should face a Final Challenge."

"A what?" asked Shelby.

"Danteri law," Calhoun told her before Ryjaan could explain it. "Danteri law is very interesting when it comes to capital cases. The state can opt to execute the criminal themselves. However, the method is very humane . . . if one can call murder humane. The only one capable of gainsaying that is the family of the deceased. They can instead demand a Final Challenge. The advantage to the accused is that, if he survives or triumphs, he can go free. If he doesn't, however, well . . . it can take several agonizing days, for instance, to die of a belly wound. Any form of killing your opponent in the Final Challenge is acceptable. The 'rare exception' I mentioned earlier."

"And as we of Thallon have a new accord with the Danteri," Yoz said, "we have agreed to adopt their laws in this matter for the time being. And your law will have you stand by and take no action."

"As I said, it's not permissible. Besides . . . I suspect that Si Cwan can handle himself. And I know that our captain is a big believer in taking responsibilities for one's actions." She looked with mild defiance at Calhoun, but all he did was nod.

"Very well, then," Yoz said briskly, rubbing his hands together. "Then we are agreed . . . the accused shall be left to our judicial system."

"Where's Zak Kebron?" Calhoun said before Yoz could continue. "D'ndai informs me he's down here."

"Yes, that's correct. As a matter of fact, he's on his way up right now."

D'ndai suddenly spoke up. "Tell me," he asked with genuine curiosity, "you have expansive, liberal views on justice when it applies to one who is not, technically, part of your crew. What if it were Kebron? What if he were accused of crimes? Would you still believe that the Thallonian standard of justice should apply?"

"Absolutely," said Shelby without hesitation.

At that moment there was a roar from the observers, and Zak Kebron and Si Cwan were brought up and into view. The representatives from the *Excalibur* were relieved to see that neither of them appeared too much the worse for wear, although Kebron did seem a bit banged up. But they were walking steadily and proud, their chins held high . . . or, at least in Kebron's case, what passed for a chin.

They were not in chains, not being dragged. There were guards on either side of them, but they seemed more ceremonial than anything. In fact, they looked rather nervous. It almost came across as if Kebron and Cwan were in charge of the moment, rather than the guards or, indeed, anyone of authority.

They moved to the middle of the room and came to a halt. They noted the presence of the *Excalibur* crewmen, but gave no overt sign, no loud greeting. The moment seemed to call for underplaying emotions.

Without preamble, Yoz said, "Mr. Kebron . . . I release you into the custody of your commanding officer. You are on probation, and asked not to return to the surface of Thallon after your departure."

Brikar emotions were generally hard to read, but even Kebron seemed to register mild surprise. Then, as if mentally shrugging, he started to walk over toward the others.

And then stopped.

He turned, looked back at Si Cwan, and then back to Yoz. "What of him?"

"He is to be handled separately. He is to stand trial for crimes against his people."

"I see."

Kebron stood there for a brief time, displaying as

much emotion as an Easter Island statue . . . and then slowly he walked back to Si Cwan, stood at his side, and faced the accusers.

Immediately more chatter broke out among the crowd as Shelby looked to Calhoun to see his reaction. To her astonishment, Calhoun seemed to be doing everything he could to cover a smile.

"Mr. Kebron, you are free to go," Yoz said more forcefully.

"I disagree," Kebron said calmly.

And now Si Cwan turned to him and said, "Kebron, nothing is to be accomplished by this. Whatever situation I'm involved with is of my doing, not yours. They merely consider you a pawn in this. Don't let yourself be a needlessly sacrificed pawn."

"It is my concern," replied Kebron.

"No, Lieutenant . . . it's mine," Calhoun spoke up. The captain was standing, his hands behind his back in a casual fashion, but there was nothing casual in his voice. "I appreciate and respect the ethics of all my crewmen. But I won't let one sacrifice himself needlessly. These people, and even Si Cwan, have released you. And you're too much of an asset to the ship for me to simply write you off if it can be avoided. I order you to take them up on their offer, Lieutenant."

This time, with what sounded like a sigh, Kebron moved away from Si Cwan and joined his captain. But he regarded Calhoun with a baleful glare that the captain did not particularly appreciate. On the other hand, he more than understood it.

"Si Cwan," Yoz intoned, "you are accused of crimes against the people of Thallon and an assortment of worlds in the Thallonian Empire. These include: suppressing a rebellion on Mandylor 5 . . . the execution of dissidents on Respler 4A . . ."

The list went on for quite some time, and Si Cwan simply stood there, no sign of emotion in his face. The crowd had fallen silent as well, every comment sounding like another great chime of a bell sounding a death knell.

Si Cwan only interrupted toward the end as he said, "Tell me, Yoz . . . do you have any proof that I, myself, had a hand in any of these activities?"

"Do you deny any of them?" shot back Yoz.

"I do not deny that they occurred. But there were others who made these decisions. I did not have control over everything that went on. Mine was but one voice. Oftentimes I learned of these incidents after the fact."

"So you believe that you are not to be held responsible. These were activities of the royal family. You were part of that family. Therefore you should be held responsible!"

"You would think that," said Si Cwan. "After all . . ." and he looked poisonously in the direction of Zoran, "if you would take the life of a young girl who had no involvement at all, certainly you would not hesitate to deprive me of my life." Zoran, hardly appearing stung by the comment, instead smiled broadly.

But now Ryjaan stepped forward, and he said, "You would deny hands-on involvement. We know otherwise, Cwan. We know of what you did on Xenex! And my bloodline calls for vengeance!"

For the first time, Si Cwan looked confused. His expression was mirrored in Calhoun's face, but since almost all eyes were on Si Cwan, it wasn't widely noticed. *Almost* all eyes, because D'ndai was watching Calhoun with undisguised interest.

"Xenex?" asked Si Cwan. "What happened on Xenex?"

"Do not pretend! Do not insult my intelligence!" roared Ryjaan. "You killed my father, and you will be brought to justice for it!"

"Who's your father?" Si Cwan didn't sound the least bit guilty. If anything, he sounded genuinely curious.

"Falkar, of the House of Edins," said Ryjaan fiercely. "A great man, a great warrior, a great father . . . and you, monster, you took him from me. From all of us, with your murdering ways."

And Calhoun felt the blood rush to his face.

His head whipped around and he looked straight at D'ndai. D'ndai was not returning the gaze. Instead he stared resolutely ahead, as if he found what was transpiring with Si Cwan to be absolutely riveting. But the edges of his mouth were turned up, ever so slightly, like a small smirk.

You bastard, thought Calhoun, even as he tapped his comm unit and began to speak softly into it. Shelby didn't notice, for she was watching Si Cwan's reactions to the proceedings.

"I have never heard of this 'Falkar,'" Si Cwan said. "I regret you your loss, but I did not deprive you of him."

"You deny it, then! All the more coward you! In the name of Thallonian and Danteri law, in the name of my family, I desire justice for your slaughter of my father!"

"Interesting justice system," Si Cwan said dryly. "Accusation is synonymous with guilt. Proof is not a requisite."

"It was much the same when your family was in charge," Yoz commented. "How many times did I, as High Chancellor, stand there helplessly while enemies of your family simply vanished, never to be seen again, while your justice would try them in their absence? At least we let you stand here to voice your own defense."

"You ask me to prove something I did not do, against accusations that I cannot address. How would you have me defend myself?"

"That," said Ryjaan, "is your problem."

And then an unexpected voice . . . unexpected to all but one . . . spoke up loudly. And the voice said, "Actually . . . it's my problem."

All eyes immediately turned to the speaker. To Captain Calhoun, one of the Federation visitors. He had risen from the place of honor and strode in the general direction of Si Cwan, stopping about midway between the accusers and the accused. Si Cwan stood there in bemusement as Calhoun turned to face Si Cwan's accusers. "Tell me, Ryjaan . . . did my beloved brother inform you that Si Cwan killed Falkar?"

"Yes . . . yes, he did," Ryjaan said slowly.

"Let me guess, D'ndai . . . you were trying to cover up for your younger sibling," Calhoun said, voice dripping with sarcasm. "Or perhaps you simply regarded Si Cwan as a useful tool for cementing ties with both the Danteri and Thallonians . . . the better to provide for you in your old age. Or maybe . . . and this, I think, is the most likely . . . you knew I couldn't simply sit by and allow Si Cwan to suffer for this . . . 'crime.' "

D'ndai was silent. Silent as the tomb.

Shelby slowly began to rise, sensing impending disaster, and she touched Kebron on the shoulder, indicating that he should be prepared for trouble. McHenry knew trouble was coming as well. However, he was also capable of prioritizing, and consequently emptied the contents of the Yukka chips bowl between his outer and inner shirt, since he had the sneaking suspicion he wasn't going to be getting any more in the near future.

"Captain . . ." Shelby said warningly.

But he put up a hand and said sharply, "This isn't your affair, Commander. Ryjaan . . . your father was not murdered. He died in combat, in war, like a soldier. He went down well and nobly. I know . . . because I'm the one who killed him."

There was a collective gasp of the onlookers. Ryjaan was trembling with barely repressed fury. "You?"

"Yes. You know of my background as a freedom fighter. You should likewise know that crimes against the Danteri were unilaterally forgiven by your government as part of the settlement of the worlds. You would stand there and accuse me of a crime that your own government no longer considers a crime."

"I have not rendered that decision!" Ryjaan said angrily. "I do not care what my government has or has not decided! That was my father who died on Xenex!"

"Yes, and it was your father who left me with this," replied Calhoun, touching his scar.

"This is a lie! It's all lies!" said Ryjaan. "You think to exonerate Si Cwan by assuming the blame for a crime you did not commit! You have no proof—!"

"No?" Calhoun asked quietly. He tapped his comm badge. "Calhoun to transporter room. Send it down."

Before anyone could react, the twinkling whine of the transporters sounded nearby, and something materialized on the floor next to Calhoun. It was a sword. A short sword. Shelby recognized it instantly as the sword that had been hanging on the wall in his ready room. Calhoun walked over to it and hefted it as comfortably as if it was a part of his own body.

"Recognize this?" he asked.

The curve of the sword, the carvings on the handle, were unmistakable.

And with a roar, Ryjaan leaped forward, his own sword out of its scabbard so quickly that the eye would have been unable to follow. *"Final Challenge!"* he howled.

"Accepted!" shot back Calhoun, and he caught the downward thrust of the sword skillfully on the length of his own blade.

The crowd was in an uproar, everyone shouting simultaneously.

"Come on!" shouted Shelby, and Kebron led the charge. He plowed through anyone between him and Calhoun, as easily stopped or reasoned with as a tidal wave, knocking anyone or anything in his path out of the way. Shelby and McHenry were right behind him. He grabbed Ryjaan from behind just as Ryjaan was about to lunge forward with another thrust and tossed him aside. Ryjaan went flying, landing squarely behind the place of honor, as Shelby hit her comm

badge and shouted, "Shelby to transporter room! Five to beam up, now! *Now!*"

And the air crackled around them as the away team vanished. And the last thing they heard was Ryjaan screaming, "Final Challenge! Final Challenge! Honor it, if you're a man, and face me, coward!"

MACKENZIE

IX.

"Captain, no! You can't!?"

Shelby and Calhoun were still in the transporter room, the rest of the away team grouped around them. Polly Watson at the transporter console had no idea what was going on, and so simply stood to one side.

"A challenge has been issued and accepted," replied Calhoun evenly. "This is a matter of justice. You said it yourself, Commander. We have to abide by local customs. The Prime Directive—"

"—is not the issue here, sir! Captain, can we continue this discussion in your ready room?"

"No." He turned to Watson. "Prepare to beam me back down."

"Yes, sir." She stepped toward the console.

"Belay that," snapped Shelby.

"Yes, sir." She stepped back from the console.

"Either you were arguing for a concept and a belief, Commander, or you were arguing for an individual," said Calhoun firmly. "It can't be that something which applies to Si Cwan or to Kebron does not apply to me."

"You're this vessel's captain," Shelby said.

"What better reason, then. I should exemplify the rule; not be the exception to it."

"If I might interject—" began Si Cwan.

"No!" both Shelby and Calhoun said.

"—or not," Si Cwan finished.

"Captain, the legality of this is questionable at best," continued Shelby. "At the very least, let's consult with Starfleet Central over the legal issues raised. You said yourself that—"

"On the first leg of our mission, you want me to drop everything and notify Starfleet so they can tell me what to do. That, Commander, sounds like an excellent way to erode confidence in this vessel's ability to get the job done."

"Permission to speak freely," Kebron said.

"No!" both Shelby and Calhoun said.

"Fine. I didn't really want it."

"Permission to return to the bridge," McHenry quickly said. "I don't think I'm serving much of a function here."

"We'll be right behind you," said Shelby.

"No, 'we' will not," Calhoun informed her. "Watson, beam me back down."

Watson took a step toward the console but eyed Shelby warily. And Shelby turned to Calhoun and said, "Captain, please . . . five minutes of your time."

He eyed her a moment. "Two. All of you out. Kebron, you look like you've been through a grinder. Get down to sickbay."

The others needed no further urging to vacate the transporter room, leaving Shelby and Calhoun alone.

"Mac, I know what this is about. It's just the two of us now, you don't have to pretend. You, of all people, can't tell me that all of a sudden you've grown an inviolable conscience when it comes to the Prime Directive."

"And you, of all people, can't tell me that all of a sudden, you don't give a damn about it."

"What I give a damn about is you, and what you're trying to prove, for no reason. This isn't about justice or the Prime Directive. This is about you needing to test yourself, push yourself. Prove to yourself that you're the man you were. But you don't have to do that! It doesn't matter who you think you were. What matters is who you are now: Captain Mackenzie Calhoun of the *Starship Excalibur*. And a Starfleet captain simply does not needlessly throw himself into the heart of danger. Let Ryjaan rant and rave. Let him nurse his grudge. It doesn't matter. What matters is that you have a responsibility to this ship, to this crew, to . . ."

"To you?" he asked quietly.

There was none of the anger in her voice, none of the edge that he had come to expect. Just a simple, soft, "I'd . . . like to think so."

He turned away from her, oddly finding himself unable to look at her. "Before I knew you . . . I knew you," he said.

"I . . . don't understand."

"I . . . had a vision of you. It's not something I

really need to go into now. I saw you, that's all, years before we actually encountered each other. I'd be lying if I said I fell in love with you at that moment. I didn't even know you. But I knew you were my future. Just as I know now that this is my future. I have to do this, Eppy. I have no choice."

"Yes, you do. And so do I. As first officer, I have a right to stop you from subjecting yourself to unnecessary risk."

"Which means this goes to the core of what is considered 'unnecessary.'" He paused a moment and then turned back to her, crossing the distance between them so that they were eye to eye. "There's a man down there demanding justice. There's only one person in this galaxy who can give it to him. I have to do this. If you claim to understand me at all . . . then you'll understand that. And understand this: I want you to stay here. To stay out of this. Do not interfere at any point. These are my direct orders to you."

Shelby, for once in her life at a loss for words, sighed, and then traced the line of his scar with her finger. "Be careful, for God's sake," she said.

"I'm not quite certain if I believe in God enough to be careful for his sake," said Calhoun reasonably. "But, if you wish . . . I'll be careful for yours."

Soleta had set up a separate research station in her quarters. She found that, while her science station on the bridge was perfectly adequate for on-the-fly research, something that required more detailed analysis likewise required relatively calm and even private surroundings. They were not entirely private at the moment, though, for Robin Lefler was with her, studying results from their scientific foray onto the planet's surface.

"You're right about these ground samples," Lefler was saying. "I'm comparing them to the results of the tests you did from ten years ago. It's similar to planting fields on Earth that have not made proper use of crop rotation. The ground has nutrients which are depleted by planting of the same crop. Thallon itself had a sort of 'energy nutrient,' for want of a better word. And the nutrients have all been drained. Except . . ."

Soleta leaned back from staring for what had seemed an eternity. "Except . . . you're coming to the same conclusion I am. That the demands placed upon it by the Thallonians themselves should not have been sufficient to deplete it."

"Exactly. I mean, this is all guesswork, to some extent. We weren't able to monitor the Thallonians on a year-to-year basis, or make constant samples of the ground. All the things that would have led to a more concrete assessment. But as near as I can tell, there's something here that just doesn't parse. And then there's that weird seismic anomaly I was picking up."

Soleta nodded and switched the data over to the readings that Lefler had picked up with her sensor web array. She watched as the blips indicating the seismic tracks arched across the screen.

"What in the world could be causing that sort of . . . of weird pulsation?" asked Lefler. "It's not like any sort of seismic disturbance that I've ever see—"

"Wait a minute," said Soleta. "Wait . . . wait a minute. Maybe we've been looking at this wrong. Computer: Attach sound attribution to seismic track.

Feed available readings at continuous loop and accelerate by ninety percent."

"Nature of sound to be attributed?" the computer inquired.

"You want it to sound like something?" asked Lefler, clearly confused. "Like what? Bells, whistles, breaking glass . . . ?"

"Heartbeat," said Soleta. "Humanoid heartbeat."

Immediately the sound echoed within the room— quick, steady, and rapid.

"You've got to be kidding," Lefler said slowly.

"Whenever you've eliminated the impossible, whatever remains, however improbable, must be the truth. Your words, as I recall."

"But this is impossible, too! You're saying that the seismic pulse we picked up—"

"—is just that, yes. A pulse."

"Aw, come on! You're not telling me the planet's *alive?!*"

"No, I'm not. Nor do I think it is. But what I think is that there is something alive beneath the surface. Something huge. That's what's causing the quakes, which are occurring with greater frequency and intensity all the time. My guess is that the energy of the planet was 'seeded' somehow, like a farmer, planting a sort of living crop. But the energy is all gone, and whatever was inside is presumably fully developed . . . and trying to get out. And when it does, whoever is still on that world is going to die."

RYJAAN

X.

THE MOUNTAINS OF THALLON were not especially similar to those of Xenex . . . but they weren't terribly dissimilar, either. This was something that Calhoun took a small measure of comfort in.

"The more things change," he muttered as he clambered up the side of a small hill to try and get a better overview of the terrain. He reached a plateau, pulled himself up onto it, and crept slowly toward the edge. The purple skies matched the color of his eyes.

The region for the Final Challenge had been selected by Ryjaan. When Calhoun had returned to the People's Meeting Hall, no one looked more surprised than the offended party, but he had wasted no time in selecting the area of the showdown. But as Ryjaan had been doing the talking—including a healthy helping of boasting and chest-beating—Calhoun had never stopped looking at D'ndai.

He passed within earshot of D'ndai as he was led past him, and in a voice just loud enough for D'ndai to hear, he said, "I have no brother."

D'ndai merely smiled. Clearly he was looking forward to having no brother in the immediate future as well.

Calhoun kept the sword gripped comfortably but firmly in his right hand as he crouched on the plateau. He listened carefully all around him, remembering that Ryjaan's father had managed to get the drop on him twenty years ago. He was not anxious to allow a repeat performance . . . although, granted, when Falkar had performed that rather considerable achievement, there had been a fairly major sandstorm going on at the time. But in this case, everything was relatively calm. . . .

And the ground tore open beneath his feet.

Just like that, the plateau that he'd been situated upon was gone, crumbling into rock beneath him as the entire area shook more violently than ever before. He had absolutely nothing to grab on to. The sword flew out of his hand, swallowed by the cascade of rock, and Calhoun plummeted, rolling and tumbling down the mountainside. He lunged desperately, twisting in midair, and his desperate fingers found some purchase that slowed his fall ever so briefly. Then he lost his grip once more and hit the ground, rolling into a ball and covering his head desperately as rock and rubble rained down around him.

And from a short distance away, Ryjaan saw it all.

Ryjaan, under whose feet the ground had suddenly shifted, jutting upward. He had clutched on to it, scrambling upward to avoid sliding into the newly created crevice, and had just barely escaped. But now he saw Calhoun, weaponless, with an avalanche crumbling upon him. It was as if the planet itself had risen up to smite him.

And Ryjaan, gripping his own sword grimly, waited until the trembling subsided and then advanced upon the buried Calhoun to finish the job.

"Evacuate?" Yoz said skeptically. "Because of some earthquakes?"

On the viewscreen, Soleta was speaking with forcefulness and urgency. "This is not merely earthquakes. You have spacegoing vessels that you use for exploration and travel. Use everything. Everything you've got. Get off the planet. We will bring up as many as we can as well. Fortunately enough, most of your population has already left ever since the collapse of—"

"We are not in collapse!" Yoz said angrily. "We will rebuild! We will be great again!"

And then Si Cwan stepped into view on the screen, and said, "No. You will be dead."

"Are we to listen to you then, 'Lord' Si Cwan? Traitor! Coward!"

"Save your name-calling, Yoz. It's nothing compared to the immediate necessity of saving our people. If you truly believe that you are acting in their best interests, you will make known to them Soleta's advice and offer. And you will do so quickly."

"You cannot tell me what to do—"

"I am not telling you what to do. I am asking you. Begging you, if that's what you want." Then a thought seemed to strike him and his tone changed into a slightly wheedling voice. "If you wish, look at it this way: This is an opportunity to make me look foolish to the people of Thallon. A nattering doomsday prophet, trying to convince them of an end-of-the-world scenario that is merely demented fiction. Those who believe and wish to leave . . . well, what use would they be to you anyway? They're faint of heart, and they clearly embrace the old ways. But those who stay with you, Yoz . . . they will be the core of the new empire that you would rebuild. They will know me to be a fraud. They will know you to be resolute and unmovable. I'm handing you the opportunity, Yoz, once and for all, to be the leader you know yourself to be."

Slowly, Yoz smiled. "Si Cwan . . . you had a knack for being persuasive as a prince. Even in disgrace . . . you have a turn of phrase. I shall consider it."

"Consider it quickly, Yoz. Because, whether you believe me or not, I am convinced by this woman's words. You do not have much time left."

Ryjaan felt a brief aftershock as he made his way toward the rubble, but it only staggered him slightly. Nothing was keeping the bronze-skinned Danteri from his goal.

He made it to the area where he'd seen Calhoun go down. The rocks appeared undisturbed. It was entirely possible that Calhoun was already dead, which would have upset Ryjaan no end. He wanted to be the one who ended Calhoun's life. He, and no other. But he realized that he might have to settle for whatever justice nature had chosen to mete out.

He scrambled over to the rock pile and started digging around. He thrust his hands deep into the rubble, searching, probing, trying desperately to find some hint or trace of where Mackenzie Calhoun was beneath the avalanche. Then he felt something, but it wasn't vaguely living matter. Instead it was hard-edged, rough. He grimaced a moment, for his arm was thrust in all the way up to his shoulder, and then with a grunt he pulled it out.

He held up the sword of his father. It glittered in the twilight of Thallon.

And then he was struck from the side. He went down, the sword flying from his hand, and Calhoun caught it. "Thank you," he said.

Ryjaan, his head ringing, looked around in confusion. "Where . . . ?"

"Dug myself out and hid, and waited for you. Ryjaan . . . now that it's just the two of us," said Calhoun almost conversationally, "I am asking you not to do this thing. It won't bring your father back. All it will do is cost you your life."

"Aren't we the overconfident one," sneered Ryjaan, scrambling to his feet, waving his sword.

"No. No, we're not. Just . . . confident enough." And he added silently, *I hope.*

"For honor!" shouted Ryjaan, and he charged.

And damn if he wasn't fast. Faster than Calhoun anticipated. Ryjaan's sword moved quickly, a flashing blur, and Calhoun suddenly discovered that he was backing up. Faster, farther, and suddenly there was a cut on his arm, and then a slash across his chest, and he wasn't even fully aware of how they had gotten there.

The son was faster than the father.

Or else Calhoun was slower.

Yes. Yes, that was the hell of it.

Twenty years ago, he had been something. He had been something great, something grand. He had reached the pinnacle of his life. And every activity in which he had engaged since then was a constant denial of that simple fact. He had been great once, once upon a time, at a time when—deep in his heart—he wouldn't have given himself any odds on the likelihood that he would reach age twenty. But now he felt old. Even though he was "merely" forty, he was old, not what he was. Not what he was at all. A mere shadow of the fighter he was.

Despair loomed over him . . .

. . . and there was a slash to the left side of his face. The cut was not as deep as the one which had created the scar, but it was deep enough as blood welled from it.

Ryjaan laughed derisively, sneered triumph at Calhoun, taunted him for not even giving him a decent battle.

And something within Calhoun snapped. Blew away the despair, burned it off like dew incinerated by a nova.

And Calhoun tossed the sword down into the ground, point first. It stuck there, wavering back and forth. "Come on!" shouted Calhoun. *"Come on!"* and he gestured defiantly, his fury building with every passing moment.

For a split second, Ryjaan wondered if Calhoun expected him to throw his own sword away. To leap into hand-to-hand combat, voluntarily tossing aside his advantage. Well, if that was the case, then Calhoun was going to be sorely disappointed, at least for the brief seconds of life that he had left to him. With a roar of triumph, Ryjaan lunged forward, his blade a blur.

Calhoun couldn't get out of the way fast enough. But he half-turned and the blade, instead of piercing his chest, skewered his right arm, going all the way through, the hilt up to the bone.

And Calhoun said nothing. Did not cry out, did not make the slightest sound even though Ryjaan knew the pain must have been agonizing. Ryjaan tried to yank the sword out.

It was stuck.

Calhoun brought his left fist around, caught Ryjaan on the point of his jaw, and staggered him. Then his foot lashed out, nailing Ryjaan's stomach, doubling him over. As Ryjaan reeled, Calhoun gripped the hilt and snapped it off the blade. He then reached around, gripped the sword on the other side of his arm, and pulled it the rest of the way through. He was biting down so hard on his lip to contain the scream that blood was trickling down his chin. As he dropped the broken blade to the ground, he flexed his right arm desperately to try and keep it functional, and then shouted, "Come on, Ryjaan! Still have the stomach for vengeance? Had enough?"

Ryjaan didn't say anything beyond an inarticulate scream of fury, and then he charged. Calhoun took a swing at him with his left arm, but the semi-dead right arm threw him off balance and he missed clean. Ryjaan plowed into him and the two of them went down, tumbling across the craggy surface of Thallon.

All around them were new quakes as the ground began to crack beneath them. But they didn't care, so focused were they on the battle at hand. Ryjaan intent on putting an end to his father's killer, and Calhoun . . .

Calhoun was looking beyond Ryjaan. Fury poured from him, savagery as intense as anything he'd ever felt, and it was like the return of an old and welcome friend. Suddenly new strength flowed into his right arm, seized him and drove him, and he lifted Ryjaan clear off his feet, tossing him a good ten feet. Ryjaan crashed to the ground and Calhoun charged toward him. The Danteri swung his legs around just as Calhoun got within range, knocking him off his feet, and the Starfleet officer was down as Ryjaan pounced upon him, grabbing him and trying to get his fingers around Calhoun's throat.

Calhoun twisted his head around and sank his teeth into Ryjaan's arm. Ryjaan howled, his blood trickling between Calhoun's jaws, and Calhoun tore loose of Ryjaan's grip. He slammed a fist into Ryjaan's face, heard the satisfying crack of Ryjaan's nose breaking. Ryjaan was dazed and Calhoun shoved Ryjaan back, leaped to his feet, and now he was atop Ryjaan, driving a knee into his chest, and he let out a roar as he drove blow after blow into Ryjaan's head. He was completely out of control, and part of him cried out in joy for it.

And then it seemed as if the ground all around them exploded.

Chancellor Yoz appeared on the screen of the *Excalibur,* and there was an air of controlled frenzy about him. "I am . . . a man of my word," he said with no preamble. "I have relayed your message to the people of Thallon and . . ."

Suddenly he staggered as the ground shifted under him. The picture wavered, and then snapped back as Yoz—acting for all the world as if nothing had just happened—continued, "And some of them have decided to take you up on your offer. They are gathering in the Great Square . . . Si Cwan, you recall the location?"

"Yes, I do." Immediately he headed over to Robin Lefler's station, describing the location in relation to the People's Meeting Hall so that she could feed the coordinates into the ship's computers.

Yoz continued, "Then you may direct your vessel's transporter beams to start bringing people up. Others are leaving by their own transports. You," and he began to grow angry, his pointing finger trembling. "You have frightened them, Si Cwan! I had hoped that they would be made of sterner stuff, but you . . . you have filled them with nightmare fears and they flee! They flee for no reason!"

"All transporter rooms, this is Kebron," the Brikar security chief was saying briskly. "Coordinate with Lieutenant Lefler and commence immediate beam-up of Thallonians at the coordinates she is specifying."

"Yoz, we'll bring you up, too," said Si Cwan. "For all that has passed between us, nonetheless this is your opportunity to save your life—"

"My life is not imperiled!" shouted Yoz. "I will not fall for your trickery, or for you—"

And then something sounding like an explosion roared through the palace. The last sight they had of Yoz was his still declaring his disbelief, even as the roof collapsed upon him.

The ground around them fragmented, tilted, and then oozing from between the cracks Calhoun saw—to his shock—magma bubbling up beneath them. It was as if something was cracking through to the very molten core of the planet. The ground continued to crack beneath them, like ice floes becoming sliced up by an arctic sea . . . except that, in this case, the sea was capable of incinerating them.

Calhoun and Ryjaan were several feet away from each other, and then the ground cracked between them, heaving upward. The ground beneath Calhoun was suddenly tilting at a seventy-degree angle. Calhoun, flat on his belly, scrambled for purchase and then he saw, just a few feet away, his sword. It skidded past him and he thrust out a desperate hand, snagged it, and jammed it into the ground.

It momentarily halted his tumble, but the impact tore loose his comm badge. Before he could grab it with his free hand, it tumbled down and away and vanished into a bubbling pool of lava.

The gap between Ryjaan and Calhoun widened, and Ryjaan took several steps back, ran, and leaped.

He vaulted the distance and landed several feet above Calhoun. He shouted in triumph even as he pulled a dagger from the upper part of his boot. He started to clamber toward Calhoun . . .

. . . and suddenly the ground shifted beneath them once more, thrusting forward onto the lip of another chunk of land. Just that quickly, the land they were on was now twenty feet in the air. There was an outcropping from another mountain that was within range of a jump, and it would be a more tenable position than Calhoun's present one, provided he could get to it.

Ryjaan started to get to his feet, to come after Calhoun across the momentarily semi-level surface— and suddenly the ground jolted once more. The cracks radiated as far as the eye could see, as if the landscape of Thallon had transformed into a massive jigsaw puzzle. In the distance, the great city of Thal— once the center of commerce, the seat of power, of the Thallonian Empire—was crumbling, the mighty towers plunging to the ground.

The jostling sent Ryjaan off balance, and he was tossed toward the edge of the precipice . . . toward it and over. With a screech he tumbled, and the only thing that prevented him from going over completely was a frantic, one-handed grip that he managed to snag on the edge. A short drop below him, lava seethed, almost as if it were calling to him. He tried to haul himself up, cursing, growling . . .

. . . and then Calhoun was there, fury in his eyes, and he was poised over Ryjaan. It would take but a single punch to send Ryjaan tumbling down into the lava. To put an end to him. The savage within

Calhoun wanted to, begged him to. And he knew that there was absolutely no reason whatsoever to save Ryjaan . . .

. . . and he grabbed Ryjaan's wrist.

"Hold on!" he shouted down to Ryjaan. "Come on! I'll pull you up!"

Ryjaan looked up at him with eyes that were filled with twenty years' worth of hatred.

And then he spat at him. "Go to hell," he said, and pulled loose from Calhoun's grip. Calhoun cried out, but it was no use as Ryjaan plunged down, down into the lava which swallowed him greedily.

Calhoun staggered to his feet, then grabbed up his sword and prepared to jump to relative safety on the outcropping nearby.

And then there was another explosion, even more deafening than the previous ones, and Calhoun was blown backward. This time he held on to his sword, for all the good it was going to do him. He was airborne, flailing around, unable to stop his motion, nothing for him to grab on to except air. Below him the lava lapped upward, and in his imaginings he thought he could hear Ryjaan screaming triumphantly at him, for it was only a matter of seconds as gravity took its inevitable grip and pulled the falling Calhoun into the magma.

Then something banged into him in midair, and he heard a voice shout, *"Emergency beam-up!"*

His mind didn't even have time to fully register that it was Shelby's voice before Thallon dematerialized around him, and the next thing he knew they were falling to the floor of the transporter room. He looked around in confusion and there was Shelby, dusting herself off and looking somewhat haggard. "Nice work, Polly." Watson tossed off a quick, acknowledging salute.

"Where the hell did you come from?" he asked.

"I was there the whole time. We monitored you via your comm badge until you were brought to wherever your surging testosterone demanded you be brought to so you could slug it out, and then I had myself beamed down to be on the scene in case matters became—in my judgment—too dire." She tapped the large metal casings on her feet. "Gravity boots. Comes in handy every now and then, particularly when the ground keeps crumbling under you." She pulled off the boots and straightened her uniform.

"You saw the entire thing?"

"Yeah." She took a breath. "It was all I could do not to jump in earlier. But I knew you had to see it through." She headed out the door, and Calhoun was right behind her. Moments later they had stepped into a turbolift.

"Bridge," said Calhoun, and then he said to Shelby, "You did that even though I gave you specific orders to stay here. Even though I told you, no matter what, that you weren't to interfere. Even though the Prime Directive would have indicated that you should stay out of it."

"Well, you see . . . someone once told me that sometimes you simply have to assess a situation and say, 'Dammit, it's me or no one. And if you can't live with no one, then you have to take action.'"

"Oh, really. Sounds like a pretty smart guy."

"He likes to think he is, yes."

Calhoun walked out onto the bridge and said briskly, "Status report!"

The fact that Calhoun was bruised, battered, and bloody didn't draw any comment from any of the bridge crew. They were too busy trying to survive. Burgoyne was at hish engineering station on the bridge, someplace that s/he didn't normally inhabit. But with the rapid changes required in the ship's acceleration, s/he wanted to be right at the nerve center of the decisions so that s/he could make whatever immediate adjustments might be required.

"We're at full reverse, Captain!" McHenry said. "I couldn't maintain orbit; the planet's breaking up and the gravity field was shifting too radically!"

"Take us to a safe distance, then," Calhoun said. "Soleta, what's happening down there?"

"The planet is breaking up, sir," Soleta replied, "due to—I believe—stress caused by something inside trying to get out."

"Get *out?*"

"Yes, sir."

The area around Thallon was crammed with vessels of all sizes and shapes, trying to put as much distance between themselves and the shattering planet as possible. The confusion was catastrophic; at one point several ships collided with each other in their haste to get away from Thallon, erupting into flames and spiraling away into the ether. Fortunately enough most of the pilots were more levelheaded than that.

"Status on the current population?"

"Most of them have managed to clear out in private vessels, sir," said Soleta. "Some chose to remain on the planet and . . ."

"Foolish. Dedicated but foolish," said Calhoun.

"We've evacuated over a thousand people onto the *Excalibur* as well," said Kebron.

"A *thousand?*" gasped Shelby. "Maximum capacity for this ship in an evacuation procedure is supposed to be six hundred."

"We've asked that they all stand sideways."

"Good thinking, Kebron," Calhoun said dryly. He turned to Shelby and said, "Looks like we'll be taking Nelkar up on their offer sooner than anticipated." Then he noticed Si Cwan standing off to the side, very quiet, his attention riveted to the screen. "Are you all right, Ambassador?"

He shifted his gaze to Calhoun and said, "Of course not."

It seemed a fair enough response.

"Sir, energy buildup!" announced Soleta.

"Take us back another five hundred thousand kilometers, Mr. McHenry. Burgoyne, have warp speed ready, just in case we need to get out of here quickly."

"Perhaps it would be wiser to vacate the area now," Shelby suggested.

"You're very likely correct. It would be wiser. However, I think I want to see this."

She nodded. Truth to tell, she wanted to see it as well.

On the screen, Thallon continued to shudder, its entire surface ribboned with cracks. Even from the distance at which they currently sat, they could see lava bubbling in all directions. The very planet appeared to be pulsating, throbbing under the strain of whatever was pushing its way out.

And then, all of a suddenly, something thrust up from within.

It was a claw. A single, giant, flaming claw, miles wide, smashing up through what was once a polar icecap. Then another flaming claw, several hundred miles away, and then a third claw and a fourth, but these at the opposite ends of the planet, and they seemed even larger. The screen adjusted the brightness to avoid damaging the eyesight of the bridge crew.

The process begun, it moved faster and faster, more pieces breaking away, and then the planet broke apart in a stunning display of matter and energy. Thallon erupted from the inside out . . .

. . . and there was a creature there unlike anything that Calhoun had ever seen.

It seemed vaguely avian in appearance, with feathers made of roaring flame and energy crackling around it. Its talons of flame flexed outward, and its massive wings unfurled. Its beak was long and wide, and it opened its mouth in a scream that could not be heard in the depths of space. Incredibly, stars were visible through the creature. It was as if it was a creature that was both there . . . and not there.

"I don't believe it," said a stunned Calhoun. "What the hell is it?"

"Unknown, sir," replied Soleta. "In general physicality, it seems evocative of such beasts as the ancient pteranodon, or the flamebird of Ricca 4. But its size, its physical makeup . . ."

"Oh, my God," said Burgoyne in slow astonishment. "It can't be. Don't you get it?" s/he said with growing excitement.

"What is it, Burgy?" asked Shelby, who was as riveted to the screen as any of them.

"It's . . . it's the *Great Bird of the Galaxy.*"

THE GREAT BIRD OF
THE GALAXY

XI.

"DON'T BE RIDICULOUS!" said Shelby. "That's . . . that's a myth!"

"Once upon a time, so was the idea of life on other planets," commented Zak Kebron.

The Great Bird, in the airlessness of space, continued to move its wings. It crackled with power. Extending its jaws, it gobbled up floating chunks left over from Thallon . . .

. . . and then it seemed to turn its attention to the *Starship Excalibur*.

"Uh-oh," said Shelby.

"I do *not* like the looks of this," Calhoun agreed. "Aren't baby birds hungry first thing after they're born?"

"Customarily," Soleta said.

"What if it moves to attack the other ships?"

"It doesn't seem interested in anyone else but us, Shelby," said Calhoun. "Probably because we're the biggest."

"Shall we prepare to fight it, sir?" asked Kebron, fingers already moving to the tactical station.

"Fight the Great Bird of the Galaxy?" said Calhoun. "Even we have to know our limitations."

The creature moved toward them, and Shelby said, "It seems to have a bead on us."

"I think you're right. Okay . . . move us out at warp factor one. Let's draw it away from the area and give everyone a chance to clear out."

"Incoming message from one of the vessels, sir," Kebron announced.

"Save it. Now isn't the time. Mr. McHenry, get us out of here."

The *Excalibur* went into reverse thrust, pivoted, and moved away from the shattered remains of Thallon, with the Great Bird of the Galaxy, or whatever it was, in hot pursuit.

"It's picking up speed," said Lefler.

"Jump us to warp four," Calhoun ordered, sitting calmly with his fingers steepled.

With a thrust from its mighty warp engines, the *Excalibur* leaped forward. The Great Bird, if such it was, flapped its wings and kept moving, pacing them.

"According to legend," Burgoyne was saying, "there can only be one Great Bird at a time. And when it senses its end is near, the Great Bird imparts its essence into a world, gestates over centuries, and is then reborn. I guess that's why it was 'mythological' . . . it takes centuries for the 'egg,' if you will, to hatch."

"But you told me 'May the Great Bird of the Galaxy roost on your planet' was a blessing," Calhoun pointed out.

"Obviously it was. Look at the prosperity that Thallon saw during the time of the roosting."

"But when it hatches, the planet is destroyed! What kind of blessing is that?"

"It's oral tradition, not an exact science, sir," McHenry commented.

"Thank you, Lieutenant," Burgoyne said.

"Sir, it's catching up."

"Pull out the stops, Mr. McHenry. Warp nine."

The *Excalibur* raced away, and this time the creature seemed to let out another squawk before the *Excalibur* left it far behind. It dwindled, further and further, to the farthest reaches of the ship's sensor, and then was gone.

There was a slow sigh of relief let out on the bridge. "Well," said Shelby brightly, "that wasn't too much of a chore."

"Collision course!" shouted McHenry.

The Great Bird was directly in front of them, its mouth open wide. Faster than anyone would have thought possible, McHenry course-corrected and tried to send the ship angling out of the way of the creature's maw.

No good. The *Excalibur* flew straight into the Great Bird's mouth . . .

. . . and out the other side of its head.

The ship was jolted, shaken throughout, and it was

all that the bridge crew could do to keep its seats. "Damage report!" shouted Calhoun.

"Slight dip in deflector shields! Otherwise we're clear!" called Lefler.

The creature appeared on their rear monitors. It appeared to be watching them go with great curiosity. Indeed, if any of the crew were given to fanciful interpretations of events, they would have said that the creature seemed just as curious about this new life-form that it had encountered as the new life-form was about them.

And then, with a twist of its powerful wings, the Great Bird seemed to warp through the very fabric of space . . .

. . . and disappeared without a trace.

This time there was a long pause before anyone took it for granted that they were safe. And then Shelby said, "Where do you think it went?"

"Anywhere it wanted to," McHenry commented, and no one disagreed.

"Captain . . . I suggest you get yourself down to sickbay. You need to be patched up," said Shelby.

"Good advice, Commander." He rose unsteadily from his chair, and found himself leaning on Kebron. "Ah. You wouldn't mind escorting me down there, would you, Lieutenant?"

But Shelby stepped in and said, "Don't worry, Kebron. I'll handle this. After all . . . if you can't lean on your second-in-command, whom can you lean on?"

"Good point," said Calhoun wearily.

"And a word of advice: Don't keep the second scar on your face. The one is enough."

"Sound suggestion, as always."

As they headed to the turbolift, he paused and said, "Oh . . . we had an incoming message? What was that about?"

"Audio only, sir. I'll put it on."

Kebron tapped his comm board and a voice filled the bridge. A voice that was instantly recognizable as Zoran's.

And Zoran said, "Si Cwan . . . I just wanted you to know . . . I lied before. Your sister is alive. Try and find her, O Prince."

And his chilling laughter continued in Si Cwan's memory long after the message had ended.

U.S.S. EXCALIBUR

XII.

IT WAS EVENING on the *Excalibur* . . . evening being a relative term, of course.

Selar was in her off-duty clothes, and she looked at herself in the mirror. For the first time in a long time, she liked what she saw in there.

She was nervous, so nervous that she could feel trembling throughout her body. For a moment she considered turning away from her intended course, but she had made a decision, dammit, and she was going to see it through.

She smoothed out her clothes for the umpteenth time and headed toward Burgoyne's quarters. On the way she rehearsed for herself everything she was going to say. The ground rules she was going to set. The hopes that she had for this potential relationship. She would never have considered Burgoyne her type, but there was something about hir that was so . . . so offbeat. So different. Perhaps that was what Selar needed. Someone to whom questions such as sex and relationships and interaction were nothing but matters to be joyously explored rather than tentatively entered into.

That, Selar realized, was what she needed. Whatever this residual urge was within her, driving her forward, it was something that needed a radical spirit to respond to. Someone offbeat, someone aggressive, someone . . .

. . . someone . . .

. . . someone was with Burgoyne.

Selar slowed to a halt as she neared Burgoyne's quarters, her sharp ears detecting the laughter from around the corner.

And then they moved around the corner into view: Burgoyne 172, leaning on the shoulder of Mark McHenry. They seemed hysterically amused by something; Selar had no idea what. Just before they stumbled into Burgoyne's quarters, Burgoyne planted a fierce kiss on McHenry's mouth, to which he readily responded. Then he popped what appeared to be some sort of chips into hish mouth, which Burgoyne crunched joyously. They side-stepped into Burgoyne's quarters, and the door slid shut behind them.

Selar stood there for a long moment. This was going to be a problem. She had counted on Burgoyne to resolve her . . . difficulty with her mating drive. Perhaps a return to Vulcan was in order. Or perhaps there was another solution, closer to hand.

Selar returned to her quarters, changed into her

nightclothes, and stood before the memorial lamp which burned so that she would remember Voltak.

She reached over, extinguished the light for the first time in two years—never to light it again—and fell into a fitful sleep.

In his ready room, Calhoun had just finished mounting the sword back onto the wall. He heard a chime at the door and said, "Come."

Shelby entered, and stood just inside the doorway. "I was wondering . . . I was about to head down to the Team Room and have a drink. Thought you might like to come along."

"That sounds great." He regarded the sword for a moment and said, "You know what was interesting?"

"No, Mac. What was interesting?"

"When I tried to save Ryjaan . . . I did so without even thinking about it. It was . . . instinctive."

"That's good."

"Is it?" he asked. "I've always felt my instincts were based in pure savagery."

"Your survival instincts were, sure. Because they're what you needed in order to get through your life. To do what needed to be done. But even basic instincts can change, and that's not automatically a terrible thing. Being a starship commander isn't just about survival. There's much, much more to it than that."

"And I suppose that you're prepared to tell me what that is."

"Of course. Chapter and verse."

"Well, Eppy . . . maybe—just maybe now—I'm prepared to listen."

"And I'm prepared to tell you, if you'd just stop calling me by that stupid nickname."

He laughed softly and came around the desk. As they headed for the door, she said, "One quick question: You told me that you had a 'vision' of me, long ago."

"That's right, yes."

"Just out of morbid curiosity . . . was I wearing any clothes in that vision?"

"Nope. Stark naked."

"Yeah, well," she sighed, as he draped an arm around her shoulder, "it's comforting to know that some instincts never change, I guess."

And they headed to the Team Room for a drink.

VONDA N. McINTYRE

THE MOON AND THE SUN

From the gifted imagination of the *New York Times* bestselling author comes a breathtaking work of epic dimensions. Part adventure story, part legend, and part gothic novel, this is a tale of alternate history so richly evocative it defies definition.

"Luminous."
—Ursula K. Le Guin

**Coming in Hardcover mid-August 1997
From Pocket Books**

POCKET
BOOKS

1252.01

STAR TREK
DEEP SPACE NINE™

24" X 36" CUT AWAY POSTER,
7 COLORS WITH 2 METALLIC INKS & A GLOSS AND MATTE VARNISH, PRINTED ON ACID FREE ARCHIVAL QUALITY
65# COVER WEIGHT STOCK INCLUDES OVER 90 TECHNICAL CALLOUTS, AND HISTORY OF THE SPACE STATION.
U.S.S. DEFIANT EXTERIOR, HEAD SHOTS OF MAIN CHARACTERS, INCREDIBLE GRAPHIC OF WORMHOLE.

STAR TREK™
U.S.S. ENTERPRISE™ NCC-1701

24" X 36" CUT AWAY POSTER,
6 COLORS WITH A SPECIAL METALLIC INK & A GLOSS AND MATTE VARNISH, PRINTED ON ACID FREE ARCHIVAL
QUALITY 100# TEXT WEIGHT STOCK INCLUDES OVER 100 TECHNICAL CALLOUTS,
HISTORY OF THE ENTERPRISE CAPTAINS & THE HISTORY OF THE ENTERPRISE SHIPS.

ALSO AVAILABLE:
LIMITED EDITION SIGNED AND NUMBERED BY ARTISTS.
LITHOGRAPHIC PRINTS ON 80# COVER STOCK (DS9 ON 100 # STOCK) WITH OFFICIAL LICENSED CERTIFICATE OF
AUTHENTICITY. QT. AVAILABLE 2,500

SCIPUBTECH

Deep Space Nine Poster
Poster Qt.____ @ $19.95 each _____
Limited Edition Poster
Poster Qt.____ @ $40.00 each _____
U.S.S. Enterprise NCC-1701-E Poster
Poster Qt.____ @ $19.95 each _____
Limited Edition Poster
Poster Qt.____ @ $40.00 each _____
U.S.S. Enterprise NCC-1701 Poster
Poster Qt.____ @ $14.95 each _____
Limited Edition Poster
Poster Qt.____ @ $30.00 each _____
$4 Shipping U.S. Each _____
$10 Shipping Foreign Each _____
Michigan Residents Add 6% Tax _____
TOTAL _____

METHOD OF PAYMENT (U.S. FUNDS ONLY)
❑ Check ❑ Money Order ❑ MasterCard ❑ Visa
Account #

_ _ _ _ _ - _ _ _ _ _ - _ _ _ _ _ - _ _ _ _ _

Card Expiration Date ____ /____ (Mo./Yr.)

Your Day Time Phone (____) - _____

Your Signature

SHIP TO ADDRESS:
NAME:_____
ADDRESS:_____
CITY:_____STATE:_____
POSTAL CODE:_____COUNTRY:_____

Mail, Phone, or Fax Orders to:
SciPubTech • 15318 Mack Avenue • Grosse Pointe Park • Michigan 48230
Phone 313.884.6882 Fax 313.885.7426 Web Site http://www.scipubtech.com

TM & © 1996 Paramount Pictures. All rights reserved. STAR TREK and Related Marks are Trademarks of Paramount Pictures.
SciPubTech Authorized User.

ST5196

COMING IN SEPTEMBER!

Day of Honor
Book Three:

HER KLINGON SOUL
by
Michael Jan Friedman

Turn the page for an excerpt from Book Three of
Star Trek: Day of Honor

And a Special Offer
from Pocket Books!

"My name is Ordagher. I am the Overseer of this station. As such, I hold your lives in the palm of my hand."

He paused, eyeing each of the prisoners in turn. When he came to B'Elanna, he seemed to linger for a moment—but only for a moment. Then he went on.

"There was an escape attempt," Ordagher continued. "Like all escape attempts, it was a failure. Still, I cannot permit such things. They are wasteful, and waste is to be avoided at all costs." The Overseer's wide mouth twisted savagely. "I want to know who led the attempt, and I want to know it without delay."

B'Elanna's heart began to beat harder in her chest. This was it, she told herself. She shifted her eyes from one side to the other, curious as to who would finally give her away.

But no one did. In the wake of the "commander's" demand, there was silence. That is, except for the throb of heavy machinery that seemed to pervade the place at all times.

Ordagher's eyes narrowed under his overhanging brow. "I am not a patient man," he growled. "Again, I ask—who led this attempt?"

As before, his question was met with silence. B'Elanna swallowed. How could this be? She wasn't surprised that Kim would stand up for her—or maybe even Tolga, with whom she had established some kind of bond.

But the other prisoners? They didn't owe her a thing.

Nonetheless, they didn't point B'Elanna out. They didn't move at all. They just looked straight ahead in defiance of the Overseer, ignoring their instincts for survival.

What's more, Ordagher didn't get as angry as the lieutenant had expected. He didn't even seem entirely surprised. But then, he was a Nograkh as well.

"You choose to be stubborn," observed the Overseer. He clasped his hands behind his back. "Very well. I know how to deal with stubbornness." He turned to one of the guards who stood behind him.

There was no order. Apparently, none was necessary. Without comment, the guard advanced to within a meter of one of the prisoners. A fellow Nograkh, as luck would have it.

Raising his energy weapon, the guard placed its business end under the prisoner's chin. Then he pushed it up a little, forcing the Nograkh's head back in response. For his part, the prisoner said nothing—did nothing. He just stood there, eyes fixed on oblivion.

Ordagher eyed the others. "Once more, and for the last time, I ask you who led the escape attempt. If I do not receive an answer, your fellow prisoner will die in the ringleader's place."

None of the Nograkh said a word. They seemed content to let their comrade perish for them. Maybe that was their way—but it wasn't B'Elanna's.

"Me," she said, loudly and clearly.

The Overseer turned to her. "You?" he replied, his brow furrowing. Obviously, there was some doubt in his mind.

"Me," the lieutenant confirmed. "I was the one who led the escape attempt." She searched inwardly for a way to back up her claim—and decided some facts might help. "One of your guards tried to rape me, and I grabbed his weapon. The rest just happened."

Ordagher shook his head. "No," he concluded.

"I swear it," she told him. She took a deep breath. "If you're going to kill someone, it should be me. No one else."

She could feel the eyes of her fellow prisoners on her. Tolga's, Kim's. And those of the guards as well. The prisoner whose chin rested on the guard's energy weapon was probably eyeing her, too.

The Overseer considered her a moment longer. Then he tossed his head back and began to laugh. It was a hideous sound, like the sucking of a great wound. Without looking, Ordagher pointed to the prisoner whose life hung in the balance.

"Kill him," he snarled.

Before B'Elanna could do anything, before she could even draw a breath, the energy weapon went off. There was a flare of blue-white light under the prisoner's chin, and a sickening snap.

Then his eyes rolled back and he fell to the floor, lifeless.

B'Elanna's hand went to her mouth. The suddenness of it, the horror and the injustice—it threatened to overwhelm her. She could feel tears taking shape in the corners of her eyes.

The Nograkh had accepted his fate impassively, unflinchingly. He hadn't said so much as a word in his defense. And all for a being he barely knew.

"Take him away," said Ordagher, with a gesture of dismissal. "And watch the rest twice as closely," he told the guards, "or the next neck that snaps will be your own." Then, glaring one last time at the other prisoners, he turned his back on them and left the chamber.

The guards took their spots at the exit. The lights dimmed. One by one, the prisoners drifted to their customary sleeping spots.

But not B'Elanna. She remained where she was, trying to get a handle on what had just happened. Trying to understand what she was supposed to do about it—what she was supposed to think.

The lieutenant felt someone's touch on her shoulder. Numbly, she turned to Kim. He looked white as candlewax.

"Are you all right?" he asked her.

She shook her head from side to side. How could she be all right? How could she just accept what had happened and go on?

Caught in the grip of unexpected anger, she

looked for Tolga. Found him at the other end of the chamber, where he always took his rest. And stalked him like an animal seeking its prey.

As she approached, his back was to her. Still, the closer she got, the more he seemed to notice. Finally, he glanced at her over his powerful shoulder, his silver eyes glittering in the light from the doorway.

"You," she said, her lips pulling back from her teeth like a she-wolf's, her voice little more than a growl.

Then she made a fist of her right hand and hit him as hard as she could. Tolga's head snapped around and he staggered back a step.

She tried to hit him with her left, but the Nograkh managed to grab her wrist before she could connect. And a moment later, his hand closed on her right wrist as well. Finally, he kicked her legs out from under her and pinned her with his considerable weight.

Left with no other weapon, B'Elanna spat at him. "You could have saved him," she rasped. "You could have said something, but you just stood there and let him die for me!"

Narrow-eyed, Tolga took in the sight of her. "Should I have interfered with Manoc's sacrifice?" he asked. "Am I a barbarian, that I should have stained his honor?"

"It was me who should have died," she railed, hardly bothering to struggle. "Me! I led the escape!"

The Nograkh nodded slowly. "Yes. When circumstances allowed, you did what was in you to do. And Manoc did what was in him."

B'Elanna shook her head. "It should have been me," she moaned. "It should have been me."

Tolga didn't say anything. He just watched her expend her outrage and her sorrow. Then he got off her and let her get to her feet.

Kim was standing nearby, ready to try to intervene if it became necessary. But it never had. At no time had the Nograkh seemed willing to hurt her, even in his own defense.

Massaging her wrists, the lieutenant looked up at Tolga. "Why didn't they believe me?" she asked softly. "Why did they laugh like that?"

The Nograkh shrugged. "Ordagher didn't believe a female could lead a rebellion." He paused. "But then, he does not know you as I do."

B'Elanna nodded. Before this was over, she vowed, she would show the Overseer just what a female could do.

Look for STAR TREK Fiction from Pocket Books

Star Trek®: The Original Series

Star Trek: The Next Generation®

Star Trek: Deep Space Nine®

Star Trek®: Voyager™

Flashback • Diane Carey
The Black Shore • Greg Cox
Mosaic • Jeri Taylor

#1 *Caretaker* • L. A. Graf
#2 *The Escape* • Dean W. Smith & Kristine K. Rusch
#3 *Ragnarok* • Nathan Archer
#4 *Violations* • Susan Wright
#5 *Incident at Arbuk* • John Greggory Betancourt
#6 *The Murdered Sun* • Christie Golden
#7 *Ghost of a Chance* • Mark A. Garland & Charles G. McGraw
#8 *Cybersong* • S. N. Lewitt
#9 *Invasion #4: The Final Fury* • Dafydd ab Hugh
#10 *Bless the Beasts* • Karen Haber
#11 *The Garden* • Melissa Scott
#12 *Chrysalis* • David Niall Wilson

Star Trek®: New Frontier

#1 *House of Cards* • Peter David
#2 *Into the Void* • Peter David
#3 *The Two-Front War* • Peter David
#4 *End Game* • Peter David